Alice-Miranda Shines Bright

Books by Jacqueline Harvey

Alice-Miranda at School
Alice-Miranda on Holiday
Alice-Miranda Takes the Lead
Alice-Miranda at Sea
Alice-Miranda in New York
Alice-Miranda Shows the Way
Alice-Miranda in Paris
Alice-Miranda Shines Bright

Clementine Rose and the Surprise Visitor
Clementine Rose and the Pet Day Disaster
Clementine Rose and the Perfect Present
Clementine Rose and the Farm Fiasco

Alice-Miranda Shines Bright

Jacqueline Harvey

RANDOM HOUSE AUSTRALIA

A Random House book
Published by Random House Australia Pty Ltd
Level 3, 100 Pacific Highway, North Sydney NSW 2060
www.randomhouse.com.au

First published by Random House Australia in 2013

Addresses for companies within the Random House Group can be found at www.randomhouse.com.au/offices

National Library of Australia
Cataloguing-in-Publication Entry

Author:	Harvey, Jacqueline
Title:	Alice-Miranda shines bright/Jacqueline Harvey
ISBN:	978 1 74275 290 7 (pbk.)
Target audience:	For primary school age
Subjects:	Girls – Juvenile fiction
	Boarding schools – Juvenile fiction
Dewey number:	A823.4

Cover and internal illustrations by J.Yi
Cover design by Mathematics www.xy-1.com
Internal design by Midland Typesetters, Australia
Typeset in 13/18 pt Adobe Garamond by Midland Typesetters, Australia
Printed in Australia by Griffin Press, an accredited ISO AS/NZS 14001:2004 Environmental Management System printer

Random House Australia uses papers that are natural, renewable and recyclable products and made from wood grown in sustainable forests. The logging and manufacturing processes are expected to conform to the environmental regulations of the country of origin.

For Ian and Sandy,
and for my mother-in-law, Joan Harvey

Prologue

Ursula turned the photograph over in her hand. His smile beamed out at her like a ray of sunshine. His short blond curls framed an almost perfect face. He had always been the pretty one.

'Two peas in a pod,' everyone used to say. 'Inseparable.'

Ursula closed her eyes and she was back there. The rain beating down, the swirling water, the log across the stream, the crack, the fall. Her hand gripping his, the screaming in her ears and the thunder overhead. Then the silence that reached all the way to the sky.

They shouldn't have been there in the first place. It was her idea. But it was an accident, a terrible, senseless accident. After the sobbing and the howling came the whispers and accusations. Her mother's finger always pointed straight towards her, while her father tried to broker peace. No one was to blame and yet Ursula felt so much guilt.

She'd left home the day after her last exams and found a job in the city. At first she wrote to her parents but there was never a reply. After a few years she stopped.

Now, almost twenty years had passed. Ursula had lived all over the world but always carried the photograph with her. She put it back in the little timber jewel box.

Ursula stood up and smoothed her trousers, then walked into the bathroom and tamed her curls into a ponytail. Life had taken some unexpected turns bringing her back to Downsfordvale. She was almost home.

Chapter 1

Jacinta Headlington-Bear could hear the girls returning from their afternoon games. She scribbled a few final words in her diary and hid the little red book under her mattress just as Sloane Sykes burst through the door.

'You missed a good game,' Sloane puffed. She slumped onto her bed and leaned forward to untie the laces on her football boots. 'We won three-nil. And I killed it.'

'Hooray,' Jacinta said sarcastically.

'What's the matter with you?' Sloane glanced over at her room mate, who was lying on her bed and flicking through a magazine.

'Nothing,' Jacinta snapped.

'It doesn't sound like nothing,' Sloane replied. 'It's only a week until you can go back to gymnastics training. You can walk perfectly now anyway, can't you?'

There was a knock at the door before Jacinta could answer.

'Come in if you're good-looking,' Sloane yelled.

Alice-Miranda appeared.

'Hi Sloane, great game,' she said. 'You should have seen her, Jacinta. Sloane flew down the field and scored the winning goal.'

'And broke a nail,' Sloane complained as she inspected her fingers.

It was a surprise to almost everyone – Sloane included – that she was becoming quite an accomplished athlete.

'Are you feeling okay, Jacinta? I thought you would have come to watch.' Alice-Miranda walked over to Jacinta's half of the room and sat on the end of her bed.

'It was only a stupid game,' Jacinta said. 'We have them every week.'

Alice-Miranda ignored Jacinta's grumpiness. 'How's your toe?'

'I don't know. Why don't you ask it?' Jacinta replied, raising her leg in Alice-Miranda's direction.

Alice-Miranda smiled at her but she had a strange feeling there was more to Jacinta's bad mood than a broken toe. She looked over at Sloane, who was pulling out some clean clothes.

There was a sharp knock at the door. Millie didn't wait to bc invited in. 'Pooh, what's that disgusting smell?' she said, pinching the end of her nose.

'Sloane's feet,' said Jacinta. 'They reek like blue cheese.'

'Do not,' Sloane retorted.

'Do so,' Jacinta bit back.

Sloane reached down to pick up her discarded socks from the floor. In one swift move she was rubbing Jacinta's nose with them.

'Get off me!' Jacinta screeched. 'You're disgusting. I can't breathe.'

'Stop it, Sloane, or Howie'll . . .' Millie began.

The door burst open and the housemistress, Mrs Howard, stood with her hands on her hips. Her bulk took up most of the doorway. 'Sloane Sykes, leave

Jacinta alone or I will have you on sock-washing duty for the whole house. Is that what you'd like?'

Sloane skulked back to the other side of the room. 'No,' she muttered.

'I beg your pardon?' Mrs Howard gave the girl a steely stare.

'No, Mrs Howard,' Sloane replied.

'Good. Now hurry along, girls. You don't want to be late for Miss Reedy and Mr Trout's end-of-year concert auditions. I trust you've all been practising something?'

Alice-Miranda beamed. 'Oh yes, I've learned a new poem.'

'Wonderful. I look forward to hearing it.' Mrs Howard smiled back at the tiny child.

'Are you coming to the auditions?' Alice-Miranda asked.

'Yes, I'm going to pop over now. You'd better get moving, girls.' And with that Mrs Howard bustled away down the hall.

'What are you going to do for the concert?' Millie asked Sloane.

'I thought I might sing,' said Sloane.

'Good idea,' Alice-Miranda nodded. 'Your singing in Notre Dame was amazing.'

Jacinta sat up and eyeballed her room mate. 'Only because she stole my part.'

'And that was *only* because you were injured,' said Sloane. 'Do you want to sing something for the concert together?'

'As if I'd want to sing with you.' Jacinta stood up and grabbed a cardigan that was slung over the back of her desk chair.

Sloane frowned. 'What's the matter? You're so crabby.'

Jacinta ignored the question and stalked across the room. She pulled the door open and slammed it behind her.

'That was weird,' Millie said.

'No, that's normal – at least, since we got back from Paris,' said Sloane.

'Has she told you what's bothering her?' Alice-Miranda asked.

Sloane shook her head. 'She's been in a permanently bad mood. I don't know what it is but she won't tell me anything. I've asked her if she's mad with her mother or her father – well, she's always mad with him but that's pretty understandable – and she didn't answer. When I asked if she'd had a fight with Lucas I thought she was going to knock me on the head.'

'She must be terribly disappointed about the gymnastics championships,' Alice-Miranda decided. Jacinta's broken toe had ruled her out of the competition, which she'd been training for all year. 'I'd be upset about that too.'

'Yeah, but she doesn't have to be such a cow about it,' Millie grumbled. 'She's got less than a month here until the end of school. The way she's going, Miss Grimm will send her off sooner.'

'Or make her repeat. That would be worse,' Sloane said.

Alice-Miranda wrinkled her nose. 'Do you think so? I never want to leave Winchesterfield-Downsfordvale. It's the best school in the world.'

'I didn't think I'd ever say this but I agree,' Millie nodded.

Sloane looked thoughtful. 'Well, it is much better than that awful school I went to in Spain.'

'I hate the thought of you all leaving and me staying on my own,' said Alice-Miranda.

'Well, you're safe for a while yet. I don't know where I'm going when I leave here anyway,' Sloane said. 'I hope it's the same place as all of you. But I suppose that's up to Granny.'

'At least you've still got another year to convince

her that it's worth spending her money on your education,' Millie grinned. 'Lucky you repeated, Sloane, or you'd be off with Jacinta now too.'

Alice-Miranda glanced at the clock beside Jacinta's bed. 'Look at the time. Come on, we don't want to be late.'

Sloane slipped her feet into a pair of sandals and followed Millie and Alice-Miranda out the door.

Chapter 2

Silas Wiley smiled for the camera. He was feeling quite pleased with himself. He'd lost a little weight recently, and even managed to put off the photo shoot until his diet was showing results. The fact that Ursula, his lovely new secretary, had commented on how good he looked had done wonders for his confidence. The photographer told him to take a break for a few minutes while he changed lenses.

Silas glanced around the chamber. He wanted to replace the shabby chairs and get the place painted.

The people of Downsfordvale deserved better than this. He knew he certainly did.

The photographer cleared his throat. 'Excuse me, Mr Wiley, I'm ready.'

'Mayor Wiley,' Silas corrected him tartly.

'Sorry, Mayor Wiley,' the man mumbled. He'd already taken about fifty shots but his subject insisted on reviewing each one and hadn't found any to his liking.

The photographer began snapping away. Silas assumed several poses, some smiling, some serious, but always looking straight down the barrel of the camera.

After another five minutes, the photographer stood up straight. 'We're done.'

'I think I'll be the judge of that.' Silas ambled over to assess the pictures.

At the same time, Ursula appeared at the door. A pretty woman in her late thirties, today she wore a striking red dress with matching red heels. Silas wished she wasn't quite so tall. With the added height of the heels, she made him feel rather like a hobbit.

'Excuse me, sir, have you finished?' she asked, smiling.

Silas waved her over. 'Perhaps. What do you think?'

Ursula scrolled through the photographs before stopping at a shot she thought was particularly flattering. 'That one.'

'Do you think so? Doesn't make me look a bit, mmm . . .' Silas pulled on his jowls.

'Oh no, sir, it's lovely.' Ursula winked at the photographer, sensing his impatience.

Silas nodded. 'All right, if you think so. Let's go with that one.'

The photographer had to stop himself from breathing an audible sigh of relief.

'How long until we get it up there?' Silas asked the man, pointing at the gap on the wall above the mayor's seat. On either side, the former mayors of Downsfordvale smiled out across the chamber.

'A couple of weeks, Mr – I mean, Mayor Wiley,' the photographer replied.

'Oh, you can do better than that, young man,' Silas said with a grin. 'Did you mention earlier that you were putting in a planning application for some renovations?'

The photographer gulped. 'Yes, sir. I'm sure that we can have the portrait back from the framers within the week.'

'Good man.' Silas slapped the chap on the back,

almost causing him to choke on the caramel he'd been sucking.

Ursula smiled tightly at the photographer. 'I'm sure he was just kidding,' she whispered, before following Silas from the room. But Ursula wasn't sure of that at all. 'Shall we get you out of that gear before your next meeting?' she asked Silas. She was amused by her boss's fondness for wearing the mayoral robes and chain. They were awfully heavy and not especially attractive, but he seemed particularly attached to them. He had even been known to turn up to morning tea fully kitted out.

Silas glanced at his watch. 'What meeting?' he barked. 'It's already half past five. You know I don't take late meetings, Ursula. What's it about – parking on the high street again? Or that silly woman with the garden gnome wittering on about next year's village show?'

'No,' said Ursula carefully. 'It's someone by the name of Finley Spencer. I tried to put him off but his secretary said it was urgent. He'll be here any minute.'

Something about that name rang a bell but Silas couldn't think why.

'Well, go and see what you can find out before he arrives,' Silas grumbled.

'Yes, of course.' Ursula turned and tripped down the hallway.

A few minutes later, she appeared at his office door. 'Finley Spencer is here, sir.'

'Already?' Silas grumbled. He was starving. The cream cheese and carrot sandwiches he'd requested for his lunchtime meeting had not satisfied him at all. 'Could you bring me a cup of tea and a biscuit? Surely Finley Spencer can wait a few minutes.' Silas paused. He couldn't think why that name had come to him so easily. Silas hated being thought of as unprofessional – what if this Finley Spencer wasn't someone he should keep waiting? 'No, on second thoughts, make a pot and get out the good biscuits. None of those ghastly honey snaps.' Silas stalked around to the other side of his desk and shuffled some papers.

'But Mayor Wiley –' Ursula began.

'Did you get any details about what he wants?' Silas flicked through a pile of new development applications.

'No sir, but –' Ursula tried again.

'Don't just stand there, Urs, go and make the tea. Give me a minute then send him in.' Silas opened the bottom drawer of his desk and dumped a stack of documents inside.

Ursula turned on her red heels and strode out of the room.

A few minutes later, there was a sharp knock at the door and Ursula entered.

'Hello, Mayor Wiley, may I introduce . . .?'

Silas stood up and walked to the door, holding out his hand in anticipation.

'. . . Finley Spencer.'

'Good Lord,' Silas's jaw dropped. 'But you're . . .' He'd been about to say 'a woman' when it occurred to him that it might not go down too well. 'Your hands are so warm and soft,' Silas said with a sickly smile. He gulped and realised that was probably quite inappropriate too.

'Good afternoon, Mayor Wiley, it's lovely to meet you,' the woman purred. She looked him up and down and smiled to herself, wondering if he wore the mayoral robes all the time or just for meetings.

Silas had never met anyone so beautiful in all his life. Her skin was like cream and her hair, the colour of honey, was swept into an elegant French roll.

Ursula interrupted her boss's staring. 'I'll just bring the tea in, shall I?'

'Yes, yes, of course.' Silas waved her away. 'Please

sit down.' He sighed deeply and directed his visitor towards the low black leather couches.

'Are you all right, Mayor Wiley?' asked Finley Spencer. She'd noticed that beads of perspiration had sprung up on the man's brow.

'Yes, yes, just need to catch my breath, that's all.' He mopped his forehead with a handkerchief.

Finley Spencer wore a striking black-and-white dress, cut just above the knee. Her black heels complemented the outfit perfectly. Silas tried not to admire how splendid she looked but his eyes were drawn to her like a magnet.

Ursula returned to the room, placed the tray down between them and began to pour the tea.

Silas offered the plate of chocolate biscuits to his visitor.

Finley shook her head. 'No, thank you, Mayor Wiley.'

'Oh no, me neither.' Silas's stomach led out a high-pitched whine.

'Please don't let me stop you,' said Finley. She watched Silas gulp and leave the biscuits on the plate.

There was an awkward silence between them, broken by Silas slurping his tea. 'How can I be of assistance, Ms Spencer?' he finally enquired.

'Well, I have a small business, Mayor Wiley –' Finley began.

'Oh, lovely, I do adore a cottage industry. A dress shop, perhaps? No, I see you with one of those day spas,' Silas prattled.

'Not quite,' Finley smiled.

Silas Wiley frowned. 'You're a hard woman to work out, Ms Spencer.'

'Why don't I just give you this?' She leaned over the table and handed Silas a small white business card.

He turned it over.

The colour drained from Silas's face. Now he knew why he'd recalled her name so easily.

'Is something the matter?' Finley Spencer was taking great delight in watching him squirm.

'I feel like a bit of a twit now.' Silas picked up his teacup and downed the dregs.

'You weren't to know,' Finley smiled.

'Yes, but of course I did. I've heard your name, but I suppose I just thought you were a man.' Silas laughed nervously. The hole he'd dug was only getting deeper.

'An easy mistake, Silas,' she cooed.

'So, how can I help you, Ms Spencer?' Silas said again. He was eager to move on.

‘There’s some land we’re interested in and I’m having a hard time contacting the owner. I thought someone of your standing might be able to assist.’ Finley batted her eyelashes as she spoke.

Silas soon forgot his faux pas. ‘Of course, Ms Spencer, I’ll do whatever I can.’

‘And you know, Silas, people are well rewarded in my industry.’ She stood up, her smile plastered in place.

‘Surely you’re not leaving yet?’ said Silas.

‘I’m afraid so. I think I can hear my ride now.’ She began to walk towards the door.

Silas tried to block her path. ‘But you haven’t even told me where this land is. I need some details, Ms Spencer.’

‘It’s all right.’ She reached into her bag and handed him a small envelope. ‘Everything you need to know is in here. I trust that you’re a confidential sort of man.’

Finley Spencer shook Silas’s hand, lingering just a little longer than she really wanted to.

Silas Wiley’s head nodded up and down as if it were on a spring. His legs felt like jelly. He watched her leave and ran to the window, where a giant gold helicopter had just set down on the front lawn.

It had already drawn a curious crowd from inside the council chambers as well as some of the local townsfolk.

Silas watched as Finley Spencer strode across the lawn, bending forward as she neared the rotors. A man opened the back door and she disappeared inside. There was a loud whumping sound as the chopper hovered and then disappeared over the top of the building.

Ursula appeared at the door. 'Can I take the tray?'

'You didn't tell me Finley Spencer was a woman,' Silas snapped as he turned around.

'That's what I was trying to say earlier.' Ursula went to pick up the plate of biscuits.

'Bring those here,' Silas ordered.

'Will Ms Spencer be seeing you again?' Ursula asked.

Silas's chest puffed out. 'Most definitely. She has given me a very important task.'

Ursula bit back a smile. 'What is it?'

'Highly confidential,' Silas replied.

'I'll leave you to your work then.'

Ursula stacked the tray with the dirty teacups and exited the room. She wondered how long she'd last working for Silas.

Silas sat at his desk and nibbled at a chocolate biscuit. He took Finley's card from his jacket pocket and turned it over.

Finley Spencer
Chief Operating Officer
Spencer Industries

'One of the richest women in the country needs my help,' Silas said aloud. He'd heard some grim stories about Spencer Industries but clearly they weren't true. Finley was the most charming and beautiful woman he'd ever met and she was using the proper pathways to undertake her business activities. Silas shovelled another biscuit down and picked up the letter.

'Now what exactly can I do for you, Ms Spencer?'

Chapter 3

Alice-Miranda was up early on Saturday morning. She wanted to telephone her mother and father before breakfast, as she knew they were heading away on business later in the day.

Grimthorpe House was still silent when she tiptoed down the hallway to the back sitting room and picked up the telephone.

'Hello Mummy,' she said when her mother answered the call.

'Hello darling,' her mother replied. 'You're up bright and early.'

'I wanted to catch you before you left. How's everyone at home?'

'All well here. How are the girls?' Cecelia asked.

'Millie and Sloane are good but Jacinta is acting very strangely. I thought she was upset about missing the gymnastics championships but it seems to be more than that. She's cross with everyone and she won't say what's bothering her,' said Alice-Miranda. 'I'm so worried.'

'How old is Jacinta?' her mother enquired.

'She'll be twelve soon. Just before school finishes.'

'Sweetheart, don't be too anxious. Sometimes when girls get a little older, they feel a bit mixed up inside. Jacinta's growing up and she's just getting to know who she is,' Cecelia Highton-Smith explained.

'Of course, Mummy, that's it. Granny once told me that I should never grow up because teenagers are the closest thing to crocodiles with a toothache she'd ever come across.'

Cecelia frowned. 'I think your grandmother was exaggerating a little bit. And who was she talking about, anyway? I hope it wasn't me and Cha!'

'One of Aunty Gee's granddaughters,' Alice-Miranda replied.

'Oh,' her mother laughed. 'Yes, Freddy's daughters could give the best tantrum throwers a run for their money. I heard about one episode where the girl spent a whole day screaming until her voice was gone and then she didn't speak to anyone for a month. But I'm sure that Jacinta will be nothing like that. Just be a good friend and let her know you're there for her if she wants you.'

Alice-Miranda nodded to herself. 'That sounds like the best idea.'

'What are you doing today?' her mother asked.

'Yesterday afternoon we had the first auditions for the Summer Spectacular and they're continuing this morning. Millie and I might go riding after that and then we're going to Wisteria Cottage to have a pizza dinner with Jacinta and Sloane and Mrs Headlington-Bear.'

'Oh, that's lovely. Give my regards to Ambrosia. And hopefully your dinner will cheer Jacinta up a bit. Please give her and the girls my love. I'm sorry, sweetheart, but I have to get moving.'

'Will you see Aunt Charlotte in New York?' Alice-Miranda asked.

'Yes, I think so,' her mother replied.

'Give her and her tummy a big hug from me. I can't wait until the babies come,' Alice-Miranda exclaimed. Her favourite aunt was pregnant with twins. 'And if you see Uncle Lawrence and Uncle Xavier give them hugs too.'

'I will. Have a good day.' Cecelia made kissing noises into the phone and then gave a little hiccup.

'Mummy,' Alice-Miranda said with a sigh. 'Please tell me you're not crying.'

'Oh, of course not, darling,' her mother said hastily.

'I've been away at school for nearly a year now and you know that I am absolutely fine and there is no need for you to be upset every time we talk on the telephone.'

'I know that, but I still miss you so much,' said her mother.

'I'll be home for a long holiday very soon – and by the end I'm sure you won't be able to get rid of me quickly enough,' Alice-Miranda teased.

'You're wrong about that, young lady. Anyway, have a lovely day. Daddy and I will speak to you next week.'

'Bye Mummy. Lots of love to you and Daddy

and everyone at home.' And with that Alice-Miranda hung up the phone.

She hadn't heard Jacinta come into the room. The girl had been standing in the corner listening for quite some time.

'Why were you talking about me?' Jacinta demanded.

Alice-Miranda spun around. 'Oh Jacinta, I didn't know you were there.'

'So that makes it all right to talk about me behind my back?' Jacinta narrowed her eyes.

'I was just telling Mummy I was worried about you,' Alice-Miranda said.

'Well, don't bother. Soon I'll be gone and you can be besties with Sloane and Millie, and you'll forget all about me.'

'We won't do that,' said Alice-Miranda, frowning. 'Is that what you're upset about?'

'No, I couldn't care less. I'll make new friends.'

'Of course you will, but we'll miss you and we'll still see you as often as we can,' Alice-Miranda reassured her.

Jacinta eyeballed the other girl. 'I doubt it.'

'But now your mother lives in the village, you can come home at the weekends.' Alice-Miranda was hoping to find the right words to make Jacinta feel better.

'Yes, but we all know that won't last,' Jacinta huffed.

'I'll talk to her this afternoon,' Alice-Miranda offered.

'Don't you dare. It's none of your business.'

'I wish you'd tell me what's wrong.' Alice-Miranda walked towards Jacinta and placed a hand on her shoulder.

Jacinta's face fell.

'Come on.' Alice-Miranda led her to the couch. Jacinta sat down with Alice-Miranda beside her. 'Mummy says that sometimes girls feel funny when they're growing up,' said Alice-Miranda. She put her arm around Jacinta's shoulder.

Jacinta stood up suddenly, as if Alice-Miranda's hand was charged with electricity.

'Well, that's not it! Just leave me alone. You and your stupid mother don't know everything.'

For the first time in a long time, Alice-Miranda had absolutely no idea what to do next. She decided to talk to Miss Grimm. Maybe she could help.

Chapter 4

Myrtle Parker opened the car boot and gathered up her grocery bags. She walked up the front steps and put her key in the door, pausing for a moment to admire her newly renovated front garden. It had always been Reginald's domain, but ever since his accident, things had got out of hand. Myrtle had despaired at the waist-high weeds and stinging nettles that lurked among her flowerbeds. When Ambrosia Headlington-Bear had moved in across the road, she did wonders on her own garden. So when she offered to help Myrtle get things in order, it seemed impolite not to accept.

Ambrosia was a surprisingly efficient worker and Myrtle excelled at supervision so they made a fabulous team. If only Reginald could see what she'd achieved, Myrtle was sure he'd be very proud.

'Reginald,' Myrtle called as she shuffled down the hallway. 'I'm home. I wish you could see the garden. The roses are blooming and the lawn looks like a bowling green but the gutters will need painting again soon. Oh, and I saw Evelyn Pepper at the store. She seems to have made a full recovery and I think she and Dick Wigglesworth are planning a trip abroad. Can you imagine? I wonder what Her Majesty will think about that?'

Myrtle had never been overseas. When she and Reginald were younger they didn't have the time or money and now, well, it simply wasn't possible. Deep down she had always harboured a dream to have a holiday in Tuscany. Myrtle shook the thought from her mind.

She went straight to the kitchen and unpacked her groceries, lining the tins up in the cupboards like an army of metal soldiers. Then she set about making a pot of tea. No doubt Raylene would have a cup –

Reginald's nurse didn't seem to be capable of making her own but she was never one to turn down an offer.

'Oh, and Reginald, we've been invited to Ambrosia's for Sunday lunch but of course I'll give your apologies, won't I?'

Myrtle poured milk into her cup and did the same for Raylene.

'Tea's ready,' she called. Myrtle sat at the small round table at the end of the kitchen. After a couple of minutes, she called out again. Myrtle wondered if the woman was deaf. Despite her earlier misgivings, Raylene had proven herself the most reliable nurse Reginald had had to date. She'd lasted several months too, which Myrtle was thankful for. The endless stream of interviews for new nurses had grown tiresome.

Myrtle set her teacup onto the saucer with a thud. She stood up and exhaled loudly. 'Good grief, woman, your tea's going to be stone-cold. I suppose you'd like me to bring it in for you?'

She slid back the glass door that led into the front sitting room. 'Raylene!' she called tersely, but the woman wasn't there. Her latest knitting project sat abandoned on the sofa and her handbag, which was usually glued to her side, was missing too.

Myrtle walked further into the room, wondering if Raylene had fallen asleep on the reclining chair in the corner again.

'Honestly, Reginald, I told her that I was popping out to the shop and she knows better than to leave you alone,' Myrtle fussed. She turned around and was about to continue upbraiding the nurse when she stopped in her tracks.

'Reginald?' Myrtle's voice fluttered like a paper bag in a windstorm and she gulped loudly. 'Reginald, where are you?'

Myrtle Parker stared at the hospital bed that took up most of the sitting room. It was empty. The machines that usually blipped and blinked stood silent. She caught sight of Newton, her treasured garden gnome, staring at her from the mantelpiece.

A wave of nausea engulfed her and Myrtle reached out to steady herself on the side of the bed.

'Well, where is he?' she demanded of her little concrete friend. But of course, if Newton knew anything, he wasn't telling.

Myrtle stood still for a few moments before taking off as fast as her legs could carry her; down the hallway, opening and closing bedroom doors, and calling out her husband's name. He was nowhere to be seen. She ran to the front door and down the steps to the driveway.

'Reginald! Reginald Parker, where are you?' she called. Her face drained of colour and she felt as giddy as a six-year-old on a carousel.

At the other end of Rosebud Lane, Alice-Miranda, Millie, Jacinta and Sloane were on their way to Wisteria Cottage to see Jacinta's mother when they spied Mrs Parker. Alice-Miranda hadn't even been sure that Jacinta still wanted her friends to go along, after their upset that morning. But when she'd asked, Jacinta had said of course she did, as if nothing had happened at all.

'Oh, no,' Millie groaned. 'I was hoping we'd get to the house without running into Nosey. She's bound to have a whole list of jobs that need doing – and of course she won't be afraid to ask.'

'Millie, please don't call her that. Mrs Parker's perfectly lovely; she's just lonely,' Alice-Miranda said.

'Seriously, Alice-Miranda, she's the biggest busy-body in the whole village,' Millie scoffed. 'I don't know why you can't see that.'

'Whatever she asks, just say no,' said Sloane. 'She can't *make* us do anything.'

'Really? You obviously don't know her as well

as Millie does,' Jacinta added. 'Mrs Parker got *my* mother – the woman who, up until a few months ago, wouldn't even touch dirt, let alone dig in it – to give her garden a full makeover. I'm pretty sure Mrs Parker could get Queen Georgiana to do her washing up if she put her mind to it.'

Millie giggled. She'd just seen a glimpse of their true friend making her way out of that grumpy impostor's body.

Jacinta grinned too.

Myrtle Parker momentarily regained her balance before stumbling down the drive into the middle of the lane, her arms flailing about like a windmill.

'I think something's wrong,' Alice-Miranda said. She ran towards the old woman.

The other girls hung back for a moment but when Mrs Parker fell to her knees, they raced after their friend.

'Mrs Parker, whatever's the matter?' asked Alice-Miranda.

The old woman's face was wet with tears. Alice-Miranda fished about in her pocket before handing over a tissue.

'Mrs Parker?' the girl tried again. 'Has something happened to Mr Parker?'

Myrtle nodded slowly and took in a deep breath.

The other girls reached the scene. 'It's Mr Parker,' Alice-Miranda explained. 'Millie, run inside and call an ambulance.'

Mrs Parker shook her head. 'No!' she said sharply. 'He's gone.'

Alice-Miranda felt as if the wind had been knocked out of her. They were too late. She'd loved reading to Mr Parker each week; he was a terribly good listener and a few times she could have sworn that his mouth almost twitched into a smile. Once, she even thought he'd giggled.

Sloane said what the other girls were thinking. 'So, he's dead?'

'Heavens, no.' Mrs Parker glared at Sloane, her lips pursed as if she'd sucked a lemon.

Millie was confused. 'So, he's not dead?'

'I really wouldn't know,' the old woman huffed.

The girls exchanged puzzled looks.

'I'm sorry, Mrs Parker, but I don't understand,' said Alice-Miranda as she helped the woman to her feet.

'Why don't you know if he's dead?' asked Sloane. 'Is he breathing?'

'I wouldn't know because . . . because he's gone.' Myrtle dissolved into shuddery sobs.

'Gone where?' Millie wondered when he had woken up. Everyone knew that Reginald Parker had been asleep on a hospital bed in the middle of the Parkers' sitting room for the past three years. He'd fallen off the roof while cleaning the gutters, broken a leg and a taken a nasty bump on the head. It had looked as if he'd make a full recovery but every day, when Mrs Parker visited the hospital and presented him with an increasing list of jobs to get done, he seemed to grow more and more exhausted. One day he fell asleep and never woke up.

Mrs Parker found it all a dreadful inconvenience. Her afternoon tea parties were ruined by having to converse with her friends over the mound of bedclothes. Nevertheless, Mr Parker had the best of care and everyone hoped that one day he would finally awake.

Myrtle scowled at Millie. 'If I knew where he was, I'd go and get him, wouldn't I? It's just like him to wake up and head straight out for a walk. Couldn't wait to leave, I'm sure – and I have so many jobs for him. Selfish man.'

'Seriously, could you blame him?' Sloane whispered behind her hand to Jacinta.

Jacinta shook her head.

'What was that, young lady?' Sloane hadn't expected Mrs Parker to have such sharp ears.

Sloane smiled tightly. 'Nothing.'

'But Mrs Parker, that's wonderful news,' said Alice-Miranda, beaming. She had been so looking forward to meeting Mr Parker properly. 'He's woken up. He's come back to you. I think we should split up and look for him. And if we don't find him, then we should alert Constable Derby. I'm sure the doctors would like to see him. It must be a medical miracle!'

'He'll need another one of those if I get my hands on him first,' Mrs Parker sniffled. 'And as for that nurse – just wait until I get hold of her. Unreliable woman!'

Alice-Miranda wondered what poor Nurse Raylene had done to upset Mrs Parker this time.

Sloane rolled her eyes. 'They probably made a run for it together,' she whispered to Jacinta.

Alice-Miranda ignored this and set about organising the search. 'I'll go with Millie. Jacinta, you and Sloane take the high street, and Mrs Parker, why don't you check the back garden and the shed? Did Mr Parker like to spend time up there?'

Myrtle Parker nodded. Her husband had spent rather too much time in the shed for her liking.

'We'll meet back here in half an hour. Make sure to ask anyone you see if they've spotted him. What was he wearing?' Alice-Miranda thought it was probably his pyjamas but she wanted to be sure.

'His blue striped pyjamas, of course,' Myrtle replied. She stared at the children. 'Well, don't just stand there.'

With that, Alice-Miranda and Millie ran towards the end of the lane. They would wind their way through each street until they met with Sloane and Jacinta. Winchesterfield wasn't terribly big and Mr Parker probably hadn't got far. Alice-Miranda just hoped that he hadn't had a relapse – if he'd lain down in a field, they might never find him.

Chapter 5

Stan Frost reached across his desk and picked up the envelope he'd collected earlier that day. He removed the letter, scanned its contents and sighed.

Another one. They were certainly persistent. He opened the desk drawer and pulled out a small pile of papers. He clipped on this latest letter, then replaced the bundle. He was about to close the drawer when he spotted something at the back. It was another bundle of letters, still inside their handwritten envelopes. He pulled them out and stared at the top one.

The words 'Return to Sender' stabbed at his heart. His mouth felt dry. He quickly returned them to the drawer and pushed it closed. Stan walked out of the little room he called his study and into the kitchen.

Two saucepans huddled together on the range, containing vegetables he'd peeled and chopped earlier in the morning. At five thirty on the dot he'd light the cooker and start dinner. Tonight he had a lovely trout fillet to go with the potatoes, beans, carrots and sprouts. A good lot of colour there, he'd thought to himself as he'd peeled the potatoes with deft speed; Beryl would have approved for sure. A tear escaped his left eye. He brushed it away, shaking his head. Just the thought of her and he went to water, even though she'd been gone for almost three years now.

It was just as well he enjoyed his own company, otherwise he could have gone a little loopy out here in the woods. He had Cynthia and the dogs, and more chickens, ducks and geese than he could keep track of. There were trout in the stream and the odd deer wandered through. He had a vegetable patch to be proud of and a couple of goats for milking. There was nothing more that he needed. He walked to the letterbox once a week to retrieve the mail. All up, life suited him just fine at Wood End. Stan picked up the bucket of scraps from the edge of the sink and walked to the back door.

Cynthia began to bray loudly. 'All right, girl, I'm coming. And where are those two little friends of yours?' He scanned the paddock nearest the cottage. Cynthia shared her patch with Cherry and Pickles, two goats she pretended to dislike intensely but could often be found cuddled up with on wintry nights. There was a small shelter in the far corner and a trough and feed bin near the gate. Cherry and Pickles charged towards Cynthia – they never missed an opportunity to eat. Stan emptied the bucket onto the ground and the little donkey and her friends quickly hoovered up the vegetable scraps. Cynthia's lower lip quivered and Stan couldn't help but laugh. It always looked as if she had something she was trying to say.

'And where are those other two little terrors? Maudie, Itch, come on. Time to go in,' he called to his two cocker spaniels. It wasn't like them to stray far from home. Stan walked around to the front garden. He could almost hear Beryl's voice: *pretty as a picture*, she used to say. The garden had been her pride and joy. Now he spent hours each week weeding and pruning, making sure that it was just so.

Stan looked across the cleared fields. Maudie and Itch probably had some poor rabbit bailed up in its burrow. He stiffened at the sight of someone in the distance. They were walking towards the cottage and it looked as if Maudie and Itch were with them. Stan walked around to the side of the building and picked up a shovel he'd left in one of the flowerbeds earlier in the day. Not that he planned to use it, but you never knew with strangers.

The figure was getting closer but Stan still couldn't see a face. He squinted, wondering if it was a traveller coming to ask for directions or a hobo.

He walked towards the low stone wall that hemmed the cottage so neatly on three sides. The frown on his face lifted when he realised the identity of his visitor.

'Well, blow me down,' Stan called out.

'I know where it is,' the other man called back.

Stan wondered what on earth he was talking about.

The fellow ducked under the rose arbour that framed the pretty timber gate in the middle of the wall. He slapped Stan on the back and smiled. 'Well, come on then, what are we waiting for?'

'Where in heaven's name have you been?' Stan asked. He led the man up the garden path and through the back door just as he'd done so many times before.

Chapter 6

Constable Derby's police car came to a halt outside Mrs Parker's bungalow. He had been as surprised as anyone to learn that Reginald Parker was missing. Surely the old fellow couldn't have got too far.

'Hello Constable Derby,' Alice-Miranda called from the veranda. 'Mrs Parker's inside.'

'Hello Alice-Miranda,' he called back.

Constable Derby trotted up the stairs and followed the girl into the house.

'Well, it's about time,' Myrtle growled as she

looked up from the steaming cup of chamomile tea that Ambrosia Headlington-Bear had just made for her. Alice-Miranda and Millie had alerted Ambrosia to Mr Parker's disappearance when they set off to look for him. She had immediately gone to see if Mrs Parker was all right. Together the women had searched the back garden and the shed and every room in the house without any luck at all. Nurse Raylene's disappearance was just as perplexing. When the children returned without Mr Parker, Ambrosia called the police.

The constable ignored Myrtle's tone, sat down opposite her at the table and took out his notebook.

'Make yourself at home, constable.' Myrtle turned and glared at Ambrosia, who was still standing near the kettle. 'Well?'

Ambrosia frowned, wondering what she'd done wrong now.

'Aren't you going to offer the man a cup of tea?' Mrs Parker sniped.

'Oh, of course. Would you like one?' Ambrosia looked at Constable Derby.

He shook his head and said a quiet, 'No, thank you'.

An uneasy silence shrouded the room.

Constable Derby coughed and said, 'Uh, Mrs Parker, when was the last time you saw Mr Parker?'

The woman set the teacup down and tapped a forefinger to her lip. 'Now, let me see. I had a very busy morning. I baked some shortbread to take over to the Fayle sisters tomorrow and then I did a load of washing. I gave my bedroom a thorough dusting and had a quick bite of lunch. Then I popped out to do some errands.'

'Did you see Mr Parker anytime this morning?' the constable asked.

'I popped my head in the door and said hello before I made my breakfast,' she said.

'But did you actually *see* him?'

'Of course I did.' Myrtle took another sip of her tea. But the more she thought about it the less sure she was.

'Mrs Headlington-Bear, you mentioned on the telephone that Mr Parker's nurse is missing too. Is that right?'

Ambrosia nodded. She'd checked the woman's room. There were still clothes in the wardrobe. And of course there was the abandoned knitting on the couch in the sitting room too. But Raylene's toiletries bag was gone.

'It's her,' Myrtle sniffed. 'She's been filling his head with all sorts of ideas. I've heard her talking about the world and all the wonderful places she's visited. She's run off with him.'

'But Mrs Parker, do you really think that's likely, given that your husband has been asleep for three years?' the constable asked.

'He's been in a coma, thank you very much,' Myrtle said. 'Reginald hasn't just been taking a nap, you know.'

'Yes, of course, I didn't mean to offend.' The officer decided to change tack. 'Do you remember the last time you saw Nurse Raylene?'

'I saw her this morning at breakfast time. She was sitting right where you are now, and she didn't stop talking the whole time. I thought my head was going to explode with all the drivel that came out of that woman's mouth.'

'What did she talk about?' the policeman asked.

'I don't remember,' Myrtle said crossly.

'But surely you can remember little bits of what Nurse Raylene said,' Alice-Miranda suggested. 'I had a lovely conversation with her about her family the last time I visited Mr Parker –'

Myrtle cut the child off. 'Well, she never mentioned any family to me.'

Constable Derby looked towards Alice-Miranda, who was standing on the other side of the table. 'Do you remember what she said about her family?'

Alice-Miranda nodded. 'Her father hadn't been at all well and she was hoping to visit him soon.'

'Did she say where he was?'

'I'm afraid not. Our conversation ended when Mrs Parker arrived home and needed some help carrying something from the car.'

'That's a pity then.' The constable glared at the old woman. 'Do you know where her family is from, Mrs Parker?'

'Of course not. It's not in my nature to pry into other people's personal business,' Myrtle tutted.

Millie could hardly keep a straight face. Nosey Parker didn't get that name for nothing. She knew more about the people who lived in the village than anyone, and she didn't mind sharing her information either.

Myrtle noticed her fidgeting. 'What's the matter with you, Millicent? Do you need the toilet? It's along the hall, but make sure that you flush and put the lid down.'

'I don't need to go to the toilet!' Millie protested. Sloane giggled and Millie gave her a death stare.

'Constable Derby, do you think we should be out searching for Mr Parker?' Alice-Miranda asked.

'We'll get to that soon, Alice-Miranda. It's important to establish just how long Mr Parker and Nurse Raylene have been missing.'

'Quite long enough,' Myrtle snapped. 'The child's right. Get the search teams together. Call in the sniffer dogs. Put out an ABC.'

'What's that?' Sloane asked.

'I think Mrs Parker means an APB,' Millie said.

'Well, what's that?' Sloane asked again.

'It means all-points bulletin. They say it all the time on American television shows when they're looking for the bad guys.'

Myrtle Parker wasn't feeling at all well. 'I think I need to lie down.'

Ambrosia Headlington-Bear offered to help her to her room and the pair disappeared down the hallway.

'What do we do now?' Alice-Miranda asked the constable.

'I'm going to alert the detectives in Downsfordvale. But with a few hours' head start, I'm afraid Reginald and Raylene could be anywhere.'

'Do you really think he's with Nurse Raylene?' Jacinta asked. 'Sounds weird to me. He didn't even know her – he was asleep.'

Sloane's eyes widened. 'But what if he wasn't?'

'Of course he was,' Millie said. 'We all saw him in there, on the bed.'

'But what if he was faking it and was awake, and then when Mrs Parker was out, Nurse Raylene and Mr Parker made a plan to get away,' Sloane prattled.

'Seriously, you've been watching too much TV,' Millie said. 'That's a stupid idea.'

Constable Derby was furiously scribbling away. He looked up from his notepad and smiled at Sloane. 'That wouldn't be the strangest thing I've ever heard.'

'See?' She poked her tongue out at Millie.

Alice-Miranda shook her head. 'I've been reading to Mr Parker every week for a little while now and I really don't see how he could have been awake and just pretending to sleep. I mean, last time I was here I read a really funny part of *Matilda* and I couldn't stop myself from laughing out loud.'

'But you said that you could have sworn you saw him smile a couple of times,' Sloane insisted. She was feeling very smug about her theory.

Alice-Miranda thought about it. She *had* said that. If Mr Parker had been awake all this time then why hadn't he just said so? And he took his food through a tube – she was quite sure that if he'd been awake he would love to have had something more substantial to eat.

Millie must have been thinking the same thing. 'But Mr Parker was hooked up to all that equipment.'

'How do you know that he was really hooked up?' Sloane asked. She'd recently started reading a detective series and was enjoying channelling its heroine. 'Did you ever see the needle in his arm or was there a plaster over it?'

Millie hated to admit it but Sloane was right. They couldn't know for sure without asking Nurse Raylene, and she seemed to be well and truly gone.

Alice-Miranda had a strange feeling that there was more to Mr Parker's disappearance than anyone knew.

'I still think we should get a search party together and have a proper look around the village and in the woods,' Alice-Miranda suggested. It's light for another few hours. Please let us help, Constable Derby.'

'I'll phone the details into headquarters first, and then how about you girls go back to school and see who you can get together?'

'What about Wally Whitstable and the fellows over at Chesterfield Downs?' Millie suggested.

'And Mr Munz and Otto at the store? Surely they could help?' Alice-Miranda said.

'What about the boys? There's a whole school of them on the other side of the village,' Jacinta announced.

'You just want to see your boyfriend,' Sloane teased.

Jacinta opened her mouth but Alice-Miranda got in first.

'Please, Jacinta, Sloane, this is no time to argue.'

'Yeah, get over it, Sloane. Seriously, who cares if they like each other?' Millie added.

Jacinta wrinkled her nose at Sloane.

Ambrosia Headlington-Bear reappeared in the kitchen. 'What else can we do to help?' she asked.

'I'm heading back to the station, but if it's all right with you, Mrs Headlington-Bear, perhaps the girls could see who they can round up and we'll meet at the showground in half an hour. I think we're clutching at straws a little but the poor old boy has to be out there somewhere,' the constable explained.

'What do you want me to do?' Ambrosia asked.

'I think you should stay here with Mrs Parker. She shouldn't be alone.'

'And then you'll be here if Mr Parker or Nurse Raylene comes back,' said Alice-Miranda.

But at that moment none of the group thought that was very likely. It seemed that Reginald Parker had indeed made a run for it.

Chapter 7

Stan Frost glanced at the clock above the doorway. It was almost time to put his dinner on; he made a mental note then looked over at the table.

'You still haven't told me where you've been,' he said.

'Home, of course,' replied the other man, who was sitting at the table. He swivelled around and patted his knee. Maudie was the first to jump out of her bed near the back door and onto his lap. 'Sorry Itch, you miss out this time.' The little tan cocker spaniel lapped up the man's attention. Itch opened one eye and closed it again.

'But that doesn't explain anything,' Stan insisted. At that moment, he wished he'd remembered to pay that last phone bill. The lack of a working telephone hadn't worried him until now.

He placed two cups of tea on the pine table.

'Have you got anything to eat?' the fellow asked.

Stan opened the biscuit tin. It was full of chocolate digestives. They were one of the few items Stan ordered in these days. He'd just leave a note and the money in the letterbox for the postman, and whatever he needed would appear a couple of days later. It wasn't that Stan didn't like having guests; he simply didn't encourage them, and since Beryl had gone, it was easier to keep to himself.

'I dreamt about it last night. I know where it is.' The man sipped his tea and took a bite out of the biscuit.

'About what? No, never mind. What I really want to know, Reg, is where have you been? And what about Myrtle?'

The man frowned. 'Myrtle?' He looked confused for a moment, as if teetering on the edge of a memory. 'Oh, she's gone.'

'I'm very sorry to hear it,' Stan replied.

Reg looked up. 'Where's Beryl, then?' It was as if talk of Myrtle had suddenly brought something back to him.

Stan cast his eyes downward. 'She's gone too,' he replied.

'Probably gone together,' Reg smiled absently.

Stan's stomach lurched. He hadn't seen Reginald Parker for three years and now he turned up as if he'd been here just yesterday. Stan wondered if living with Myrtle all those years had knocked the sensitivity right out of the silly old fool. Surely he'd heard that Beryl had died. The funeral had been a private affair: just the priest, Maudie, Itch and Stan, exactly as Beryl had requested. No family, no added complications. Even so, word got around the village and Stan had been surprised to find several casseroles and cakes left on the doorstop at the house. Reg must have known.

Stan spoke again. 'What did you do to your arm?' He pointed at the sticking plaster covering Reg's wrist.

He looked at it and shrugged. 'I don't know.' Reg drank his tea, savouring every last drop. 'Geez, these biscuits are delicious,' he enthused, reaching out to take another.

'You never liked them much before.' Stan watched as Reg devoured at least six of them. 'Haven't you eaten today?'

Little did Stan know that Reginald Parker hadn't eaten a piece of solid food in years.

Reginald gave Maudie a gentle prod and she leapt down from his lap. He walked to the sink, rinsed out his teacup, and looked expectantly at Stan. 'Well, come on then, we should get out there.'

'Out where?' said Stan.

'What's wrong with you, Stanley Frost? Have you forgotten that we're on the verge of making a huge discovery? We'll be famous the length and breadth of the county. If we tell anyone, that is. I'd rather we kept it to ourselves for now. Anyway, I dreamt where we'll find it.'

The penny suddenly dropped. 'I haven't been up there in years,' Stan whispered.

'What do you mean, Stan? We were there yesterday and the day before that and the day before that.'

Stan Frost shook his head. Something had happened to his friend. Something terrible. He needed to get to the village and let someone know. Reginald Parker had gone mad. Or Myrtle had driven him to it. The last time he'd seen Reg, he said that he had to get home and clean out the gutters because Myrtle would be back soon and she'd have his guts for garters if it wasn't done. Stan hadn't seen the old girl in years but he'd suffered often enough at her hands to know that Reg probably wasn't kidding. He waited the next day for him to reappear. And the day after that. He'd telephoned the house several times but there was no answer. And then a week passed and a month. He'd wanted to go into the village to look for him but Beryl was insistent. There was never any good to come out of his friendship with Reg Parker, she said. Just leave things alone.

And so he had, until he made one last call just before Beryl got sick. Myrtle had answered and when Stan asked to speak to Reg, she replied tartly that Mr Parker wasn't in the business of speaking with anyone these days and promptly hung up the phone. She hadn't asked who it was and Stan didn't say. So that was that. Beryl's illness and sudden death had knocked Stan sideways. Afterwards, he just puddled along on his own with the animals and his memories to keep him company. But why had Reg come back after all this time, and why did he think he'd been there the day before?

'We need to go to the village,' Stan said, wishing he'd kept up a bit more maintenance on the old Cortina in the shed and the bridge over the stream. He hadn't turned the engine over in more than a year. If they were to go anywhere it would be on foot.

'Bah, I'm not going to the village. Come on, Stan. We've got work to do. Let's get outside and have a look. You won't be sorry.'

But Stan found that hard to believe. Reg walked over to the back door and grabbed the large torch that hung by a strap from the old hat stand. 'What are you waiting for? An invitation?'

Stan walked over to join him.

'That's the spirit. You wait, Stan. This is it. The big one. I can feel it in my bones.' Reg Parker walked out the door and into the back garden. He turned to look at his friend. 'And Stan, I think I might stay here tonight, if that's all right with you.'

Stan shrugged. He wondered how many more surprises there could possibly be before nightfall.

Chapter 8

'What a dreadful situation.' Doreen Smith looked up from the pot where she was fishing red frankfurts from the boiling water. The girls were having hot dogs as a weekend treat, although Doreen wondered at the word 'treat'. Hot dogs never failed to give her a jolly good dose of indigestion.

'I just hope that wherever he is, Mr Parker's all right,' Alice-Miranda said as she plonked the frankfurts into bread rolls. The production line was completed by Millie, who was running a streak of tomato sauce down the centre of each roll.

'Well, I'm sure the police will do everything they can,' said Mrs Smith.

Millie looked up from her job and frowned. 'You know Mrs Parker's not my favourite person in the world, but what's happened to her is awful. Imagine having your husband in a coma for all those years and then suddenly he disappears.'

'I couldn't agree more,' Mrs Smith nodded. 'What a shock. And that Nurse Raylene – I met her at the Munzes' store just the other afternoon and she seemed like such a nice woman.'

'We still don't know for sure if they've gone off together,' Alice-Miranda said. 'It could just be a coincidence.'

'A very unlikely one I'd say, but you're right, Alice-Miranda. We shouldn't go jumping to conclusions. I'm sure that Myrtle's done enough of that for all of us.' Mrs Smith carried the enormous saucepan to the sink and set it down.

'No, Sloane's got the best imagination there,' said Millie. 'She decided that Mr Parker must have been faking it for ages and that he and Raylene had it planned all along.'

Mrs Smith shook her head and caught sight of the kitchen clock. 'Goodness me, look at the time.' It was almost nine. She couldn't remember ever feeding the girls as late as that. 'Are you almost done there, Millie?' The child nodded. 'Well come on, let's wheel that trolley through before we have anarchy on the other side.'

Alice-Miranda held open the swing doors that led from the kitchen through to the dining room. The girls were seated at the tables chatting away, but Mrs Smith noticed immediately that the emergency biscuit jar looked rather depleted.

Alice-Miranda and Millie made their way to where Jacinta and Sloane were sitting. Miss Reedy had brought the girls back to school while the rest of the teachers had stayed in the village to continue the search.

Now, she stood up on the podium to direct the dinner traffic. 'Good evening, girls.'

Within a couple of seconds the room was silent.

'May I first say thank you to everyone for your assistance this evening in the search for Mr Parker. We all hope and pray for his safe return home. And of course I will let you know as soon as we hear anything.'

'Miss Reedy, why did the Fayle boys get to stay out while we had to come back?' Jacinta called.

The English teacher glared at Jacinta. 'Professor Winterbottom was in charge there and so it was up to him. I think the boys had had a late barbecue lunch, unlike you girls, who must be starving by now.'

Jacinta pouted. She'd been having a lovely time talking to Lucas about their trip to Paris and wasn't the least bit impressed when the girls had been told to go back to school.

'Now, Mrs Smith has prepared hot dogs for your dinner and I do believe that I smelt some treacle puddings for dessert, but we are very late so you mustn't dally. You need to be in bed by ten o'clock. The girls in the sixth grade who are going to Sainsbury Palace School next year must be on the bus and ready to leave for their orientation day by nine tomorrow. Mr Plumpton and I will be accompanying you over to Downsfordvale.'

'Oh, what fun.' Jacinta's voice was dripping with sarcasm.

'We wish you didn't have to go either, Jacinta.' Alice-Miranda reached up and put her hand on Jacinta's shoulder.

'Speak for yourself,' said Millie, pulling a face.

'Millie! You don't mean that,' Alice-Miranda scolded.

The flame-haired child smiled. 'No.' She almost seemed surprised. 'I didn't mean that. Who'd have thought it, Jacinta? I wish you could stay too.'

'Who said I wanted to?' Jacinta poked her tongue out at Millie.

'I'll have a new room mate next year,' Sloane said absently. 'Maybe she'll actually know how to put her underwear away.'

'And maybe I'll get some sleep,' Jacinta shot back. 'I couldn't possibly end up with someone who snores as loudly as you.'

'I do not!' Sloane snapped.

'Do too!' said Jacinta, her eyes narrowed.

'Come on, you two, be kind,' Alice-Miranda implored. 'I'd say you make a pretty good team, even if you don't realise it.'

'Sainsbury Palace has an amazing gym program. They've had lots of champions,' Millie said. 'And it'll only be a year before Sloane and I start there too.'

'Great,' Jacinta mumbled.

Miss Reedy clapped her hands to get everyone's attention. 'All right, girls, I think we should let the sixth graders go first tonight.' She looked at the group in front of her, and felt a twinge of sadness to be losing these wonderful girls. Danika had proven herself a most capable and reliable leader, and all up they were a lovely bunch. Some years, she couldn't wait to see the back of the oldest students – they could get quite difficult towards the end. This year would have been the same had Alethea Goldsworthy not departed when she did, but without her influence they really were super.

Jacinta stayed in her seat.

Alice-Miranda nudged her friend. 'You should go up.'

Jacinta shuddered. 'I'm not eating that rubbish. I hate hot dogs.'

'Well, there's some salad,' Alice-Miranda suggested.

'I'm not hungry,' Jacinta grumbled.

'Really? I could eat a horse,' Alice-Miranda said. 'Well, maybe not a horse, but you know what I mean. Are you sure?'

'I don't want anything,' Jacinta snapped. 'We were supposed to be having pizzas at my mother's place, remember? Until stupid Mr Parker went and ran away.'

'Jacinta,' Alice-Miranda said, 'are you okay?'

'I'm fine. Stop asking, will you?' Jacinta jumped up and stormed off.

Alice-Miranda frowned.

'Don't worry about her. She's probably just tired and hungry and won't admit it,' Millie said.

'She's cranky that she had to leave her boyfriend.' Sloane smirked. 'Didn't you see her and Lucas at the showground?'

'They were just the same as always,' said Millie. 'Jacinta was mooning all over him and Lucas was ignoring her.'

But Alice-Miranda didn't think so. Lucas had seemed different. Instead of blushing and trying to steer clear of Jacinta he had walked straight up and asked how her toe was and if she was feeling okay. And when they were in Paris he'd insisted on accompanying her to the hospital with Alice-Miranda and her mother.

The rest of the girls were directed to the servery, and the teachers and other staff arrived back from the search in time to eat too.

'Is there any news, Mr Plumpton?' Alice-Miranda asked the Science teacher as he passed their table.

'No,' he answered. 'I'm afraid they've called off the search for the night. Tomorrow they'll bring in reinforcements and I heard Constable Derby telling someone about the police rescue helicopter and sniffer dogs too.' He was looking over Alice-Miranda's shoulder and seemed anxious to get away.

'Did Mrs Parker join the search?' Millie asked.

'No, I think she stayed at home with Mrs Headlington-Bear looking after her,' Mr Plumpton explained. 'If you'd excuse me, Millie, I need to see Miss Reedy quite urgently.'

Millie turned and grinned at Alice-Miranda. 'They're so cute.'

'Adorable,' Alice-Miranda replied. But she knew a little more than the other girls. Mr Plumpton had taken Miss Reedy on a very special dinner the last night of their trip in Paris. Alice-Miranda had overheard the two of them talking about it. When they realised she was there, they'd sworn her to secrecy.

Alice-Miranda was hopeful that there would be another wedding sometime soon.

The girls took their meals back to the tables and devoured the hot dogs and puddings in record time.

'We should take Chops and Bonaparte out tomorrow and see if we can help with the search,' Millie suggested.

Alice-Miranda nodded. 'Good idea.'

'Count me out,' said Sloane.

'You could go on foot, Sloane,' Alice-Miranda said.

'Oh, I suppose so. I'm just not going near those horrible horses.' Sloane shuddered. She still hadn't got over her last riding experience, when Stumps bolted for home.

'Let's go back to the house,' Millie said.

'I'll just pop into the kitchen and see if Mrs Smith has something I can take back for Jacinta,' said Alice-Miranda. 'She can't survive on fresh air.'

Millie offered to wait but Sloane left with another group of girls to walk the short distance from the dining room to Grimthorpe House. She thought she'd probably find Jacinta already in bed.

Chapter 9

'And just where do you think you're taking that?' demanded Mrs Howard. She had been patrolling the hallways at Grimthorpe House and directing the girls to their showers or to brush their teeth and get straight to bed.

'Oh, hello Mrs Howard,' Alice-Miranda greeted the housemistress. 'Mrs Smith made Jacinta a cheese sandwich because she didn't eat any dinner. May I give it to her? I know she'll have to brush her teeth again but she must be starving and she has to be up early for the orientation day tomorrow.'

Mrs Howard's forehead wrinkled. 'I haven't seen Jacinta come in.'

'But she left the dining room ages ago, before we had our treacle puddings,' Millie said. 'Maybe you were upstairs.'

Mrs Howard nodded. Yes, perhaps that was it. She'd ducked up to get some thread to finish the baby blanket she was making for her new grandchild.

'Take it to her room and tell her that I will not be pleased if I find a mountain of crumbs in her bed in the morning,' Howie growled.

'Will do,' Alice-Miranda smiled. 'Goodnight, Mrs Howard.'

'Goodnight, Howie,' Millie added.

'I'll be along shortly for lights out,' the woman said, rubbing her stiff neck. She was getting far too old for all this.

Alice-Miranda knocked gently on Jacinta and Sloane's door. There was no answer. She opened it and was surprised to find the room empty. She'd thought Jacinta might be there but refusing to answer. Although Jacinta had come a very long way over the past year, there were still occasional glimmers of the girl who'd earned herself the tag of school's second best tantrum thrower.

Millie had already changed into her pyjamas when Alice-Miranda walked into their room next door.

'I think Jacinta must be in the bathroom,' the child said as she flopped onto her bed. 'I left the sandwich on her bedside table.'

Millie grabbed her toiletries bag and headed for the door. 'I'll tell her when I see her.'

Alice-Miranda changed into her pyjamas too and went to brush her teeth. The bathroom was steaming from the steady stream of showers. She stood at the sink beside Millie, who had a mouthful of foam.

'Did you see Jacinta?' Alice-Miranda asked.

Millie shook her head and spat into the basin. 'Uh-uh, she wasn't in here – unless she's in the shower.' Millie walked along the row of cubicles, poking her head under the doors to see if she could recognise any of the inhabitants' legs.

'None of those ankles are skinny enough for Jacinta,' she declared.

'Excuse me, I heard that,' Sloane yelled from the end shower. 'I've got very dainty ankles. My mother said so.'

'Really?' Millie giggled. 'And you'd believe a word she says?'

'Leave my mother alone,' Sloane snapped. 'She's not always wrong.' She emerged from one of the shower cubicles wrapped in a towel. Her long blonde hair dripped all over the floor.

'I don't understand you, Sloane. You say awful things about your mother all the time and the minute someone makes a joke, you're all over them like a wet rag,' Millie complained.

Sloane rolled her eyes. 'I can say it because she's *my* mother.'

Mrs Howard bustled into the room and almost slipped on a puddle that Sloane had created.

'Why is your hair wet? the housemistress growled. She had been stalking the hallways telling the girls to hurry along, and realised that there was still far too much activity in the lower bathroom.

'Because I washed it,' Sloane said. Wasn't that obvious? She wondered if Howie was losing her marbles.

'There's no need to get smart with me, young lady.' Howie was clearly not happy. 'You do realise that it's almost ten o'clock and I expect you to be in bed with lights out in ten minutes? How do you plan to dry it before then?'

Sloane hadn't really thought of that and she'd quite forgotten how late it was.

'I've got a hair dryer.' She squeezed the excess moisture out of her long mane, creating another gush of water on the floor.

'Sloane Sykes, you will not keep the rest of the house awake with that supercharged turbo monstrosity of yours.'

It was true that Sloane's hair dryer resembled a jet engine and was about as loud as one too.

'But I can't go to bed with wet hair,' Sloane whined. 'I'll catch pneumonia and then it will be all your fault.'

'Don't you dare threaten me, madam. One word to Miss Grimm and you'll be back in Spain for good.'

Sloane gulped.

'I have a hair dryer in my room, Mrs Howard. It's very quiet,' Alice-Miranda offered. 'I can help Sloane with her hair.'

'I don't see why you should have to be up any later either.' Now Mrs Howard glowered at Alice-Miranda and Millie.

'Thank you,' Sloane mouthed to the smaller girl.

'And where is Miss Headlington-Bear?' Mrs Howard asked. 'Did you find her?'

Millie and Alice-Miranda shook their heads. 'I think she must have gone to her room when I went to the toilet,' said Alice-Miranda.

'She wasn't here when I got back,' Sloane said.

'Where on earth could the child be?' Mrs Howard grumbled. 'Right, Alice-Miranda, you go and have a look in the sitting room. Millie, you take the upstairs bathroom and bedrooms and I'll do a sweep of all the bedrooms down here,' Mrs Howard instructed.

'What about me?' Sloane asked.

'You can take yourself straight to Alice-Miranda's bedroom and get that hair dried,' Howie snapped, before turning on her heel and marching towards the door.

Sloane's tongue shot out of her mouth.

'Excuse me young lady, what was that?'

Sloane recoiled. She closed her mouth quick smart and wondered if Howie really did have eyes in the back of her head.

☆

Alice-Miranda scooted along the hallway to the sitting room at the back of the house. She checked all the couches – girls had been known to fall asleep on them in front of the television and be completely overlooked at bedtime – but Jacinta wasn't there. Millie searched every room upstairs to no avail either. The only place she didn't look was Howie's flat, but it was strictly off limits to the girls unless specifically invited. Millie could only remember one time that Howie had asked her in – when she'd been helping her carry some parcels upstairs. Heaven help Jacinta if she was in there.

Mrs Howard puffed and blew as she bustled along the hallway, walking in and out of bedrooms, saying goodnight to the girls and snapping the lights off as she left. She was also checking for Jacinta but didn't want to ask the girls lest they get worked up. And no one wanted girls worked up at that time of night.

There was no sign of Jacinta anywhere. Mrs Howard headed back to the girl's own room just to be sure that none of them had missed her in their rushing about. At that moment, Millie scurried downstairs, almost bowling Alice-Miranda over at the bottom.

'Did you find her?' Millie asked.

Alice-Miranda shook her head.

'Me neither,' said Millie. The girls scooted along towards their room. Mrs Howard was now standing in the doorway and the hair dryer whirred inside.

'In you go,' the housemistress directed the two children.

Sloane turned around from the mirror. 'I'm nearly finished. I promise.'

'Never mind about that.' Mrs Howard looked at Alice-Miranda and Millie. 'I gather since you've come back unaccompanied that neither of you has managed to locate Jacinta.'

They shook their heads in unison.

'Well, dear me.' Mrs Howard wrung her hands together. 'I think it's time to call Charlie and see if he can have a look around the grounds. Can you think of anywhere she might have gone?'

The girls shook their heads again.

'Maybe she walked to her mother's place,' Sloane said. 'She was going on about how she hated hot dogs and we were supposed to have pizzas at Wisteria Cottage tonight.'

'I'm sure that Jacinta wouldn't have gone without asking,' said Alice-Miranda staunchly, although secretly she was worried.

'If she's walked back to the village on her own at

this time of night, there will be trouble, I can assure you.' Mrs Howard's crossness belied the fact that she was worried too. She'd never lost a girl on her watch and she didn't want to start now. It seemed that Reginald Parker and Nurse Raylene weren't the only ones missing that night.

Chapter 10

'A walk, that's all,' Reginald Parker had said. But it seemed he had more than a simple walk in mind. He and Stan had faffed about in the garage to find the old headlamps and some gear.

Stan Frost suspected it was a waste of time. He had no idea if they'd even be able to get inside. There'd been a lot of rain last year and he'd noticed a few mudslides on the mountain. The entrance to the cave might have been covered up by now. Part of him hoped it was.

Stan and Reg ambled along in the late sunshine. When they reached the bottom of the hillside, Stan was surprised to find himself ahead of his friend. It had taken Reg much longer to navigate the narrow trail that led steeply to the cave's entrance. Several times Reg grasped at the vegetation to steady himself and had to stop to catch his breath. Stan couldn't remember his friend ever being this slow before. He was different too, although Stan couldn't exactly say how.

'Are you all right?' Stan asked Reg, and offered him a hand to get up a particularly steep part of the track.

'Right as rain, Stan. Can't think why I'm so tired though. I've never been this slow in my life.' Reg steadied himself. 'Look, Stan, there she is.' He pointed then knocked on his hard hat – it was something he'd always done before they went inside. Reg switched on the amber glow of the headlamp and pushed his way through the waterfall of vines that had sprouted from above, shielding the entrance like a bridal veil.

'Where'd this lot come from?' Reg asked as he parted the long tendrils. 'Must be the fastest growing creeper on earth.'

Stan wondered what he was talking about. Reg

led the way inside. Stan followed. The cave was just as he remembered. A dank smell rose up and assaulted his nostrils and the glow from their headlamps sent a small colony of bats screeching towards the entrance.

Stan was terrified that the bats would turn around and fly back towards them. He'd never much liked the little blighters with their big ears.

Reg traced the walls of the cave for hours, his nose almost pressed up against the surface at times.

Stan searched too but he didn't like their chances of finding anything. Although he had stumbled upon a few small treasures once, many years before, they'd been up there hundreds of times since and never come across anything except the odd lizard, and of course the bats. Then again, it had always been the thrill of the chase more than anything else. Stan's stomach grumbled. He looked down at his watch, shining the headlamp onto its face. It had just gone ten o'clock. Four hours after his appointed dinnertime.

'Come on, Reg, let's pack it in for the night,' he called out. 'I don't know about you but I'm starving.'

Reg was feeling light-headed himself but had put it down to being in the confined space. 'All right. But tomorrow'll be the day. You mark my words.'

Stan wondered if Maudie and Itch might have demolished the kitchen looking for their dinner. He hadn't planned on being out so long.

By the time they reached the bottom of the hillside and started across the field for home, Stan had decided that he wanted some answers.

'Reg, I need to know exactly where you've been for the past three years.' The headlamp on Stan's helmet glared into Reginald's grey eyes. Stan thought they looked strangely hollow – almost empty.

Reg frowned. 'I don't know what you're talking about, Stan. I was here yesterday.'

'Stop it, Reg. Three years ago you left here one afternoon and said that if you didn't get home and get the gutters cleaned out, Myrtle would string you up. Then you disappeared and I haven't seen you since then until today.'

Reg shook his head. 'I think you're losing your marbles, old friend – too much time in the woods.'

Stan didn't know what else to say, so he clammed up. When they reached the cottage, Reg followed Stan through the back door.

He went straight to the stove, lit a match and threw it in with the kindling that he had ready inside. Then he ducked through to the utility room and organised some mincemeat for the dogs, who were dancing about at his knees.

Reg sat down at the kitchen table.

Stan retrieved two fillets of fish from the fridge. He'd been planning to have them for the next couple of nights but now they'd do for both of them.

'Dinner will be a while,' he said. When he turned around, Reginald seemed to have drifted off to sleep.

Chapter 11

'Please, Mrs Howard, can Millie and I help Mr Charles search for Jacinta? The school's so big and there are loads of places that she could have gone.' Alice-Miranda looked pleadingly at the old woman, who was hovering next to the telephone in the sitting room. She'd already called Charlie Weatherly, the school gardener, half an hour ago and the trio were now anxiously awaiting any news.

Howie shook her head. 'It's far too late to have you two wandering about.' She wondered what had got into Jacinta. She used to be a right terror but since she'd been befriended by Alice-Miranda she'd become quite the model student. This was most definitely a backward step.

'Shouldn't you telephone Mrs Headlington-Bear and see if Jacinta walked over to Wisteria Cottage?' Millie said.

'Millicent, the poor woman has had enough trauma for one day without me adding to her worries. And I suspect she's looking after Mrs Parker this evening, which is more suffering than anyone should have to bear.'

Millie smiled. Howie was right about that.

'But what if Jacinta turns up there and her mother telephones you first and then you'll have to explain why you didn't tell her that Jacinta was missing.'

Howie rubbed her chin. She hadn't thought of that. She imagined that Ambrosia Headlington-Bear would become hysterical when she found out what was going on.

'Mrs Howard, I have an idea where Jacinta could be,' said Alice-Miranda.

The telephone rang and the old woman almost shot through the ceiling. She snatched the handset from the cradle.

'Hello, Charlie, what news?'

Alice-Miranda and Millie looked up at her expectantly.

'Oh dear. No sign?'

There was a long pause as Charlie explained where he'd searched.

'I think we have to alert her mother in case she's gone there – although I would have expected the woman to call if the child had turned up.'

There was another lengthy silence.

'All right, I'll telephone Miss Grimm instead, and you contact Constable Derby.' Mrs Howard gulped. 'Hold on a minute, Charlie –' She looked at Alice-Miranda. 'Do you really think you know where she might be?'

'Yes, we can be there and back in ten minutes.' Alice-Miranda grabbed Millie's hand and together they were halfway out the door before Mrs Howard had time to object.

'Hold off, Charlie. I'll call you back.' Mrs Howard hung up and began to pace up and down the room.

She glanced at the clock on the wall. It was almost eleven.

'Where are we going? Millie asked as Alice-Miranda charged up the driveway.

It was fortunate there was a full moon lighting their path, as neither of the girls had thought to grab a torch.

'The stables?' said Millie, as she realised where they were heading. 'But Jacinta hates horses. I don't remember her ever coming up here.'

'Exactly,' Alice-Miranda said. 'No one would think to look for her here.'

The girls scurried into the cool brick building and Alice-Miranda flicked on the overhead lights. Bonaparte nickered softly.

'Sorry, Bony, I didn't mean to wake you up,' she said.

The pony threw his head over the stall door and bared his teeth.

Millie went from stable to stable, hauling herself up to look inside, although she couldn't imagine that Jacinta would go in with any of the horses. She was terrified of them.

Alice-Miranda went to the tack room, then to the feed room, and returned with a treat for Bonaparte.

'Consider this an apology.' She held out the carrot and he hoovered it up.

'She's not here,' said Millie, shaking her head.

'What about up there?' Alice-Miranda pointed.

'There's no one in the flat since Billy moved out.'

Millie nodded. She opened the door and scampered up the stairs, with Alice-Miranda close behind.

The place looked just as it had when Billy Boots had lived there for a short while, before the girls learned that he was really Liam Sharlan, the rightful owner of the carnival that came each year to the village for the show. The new stablehand, a girl called Elsa, was taking a gap year before university and lived with her parents on a farm a few miles away.

The lounge room was empty. Alice-Miranda walked to the far end of the room and opened the bedroom door.

'Jacinta!' she exclaimed and ran towards the bed. The girl was fast asleep.

Millie raced in and stood beside Alice-Miranda, then reached out and prodded Jacinta's shoulder.

'What?' The girl woke with a start.

'What are you doing up here?' Alice-Miranda was wide-eyed. 'Mrs Howard is about to call the police.'

'The police?' Jacinta wondered what she was talking about. 'What's the time?'

'It's after eleven,' Millie said.

'Eleven?' Jacinta repeated.

'Come on, we've got to get back to the house.' Alice-Miranda grabbed Jacinta's hand to help her off the bed.

'But *what are* you doing up here?' Millie tried again.

Jacinta frowned. 'I don't want to talk about it.'

'Well, you'd better think of something to say, because I'm pretty sure that Mrs Howard will want to talk about it.'

Jacinta pouted. 'I don't care.'

'What's the matter?' Alice-Miranda asked. 'I don't understand why you got so cross about the hot dogs. I mean, I know you were disappointed about us not having pizzas with your mother but that can't be the reason you ran off. I'm sure that once we find Mr Parker we can arrange another pizza night.'

'Just stop talking!' Jacinta stalked ahead of the two girls, stomping downstairs and into the stable block below.

Millie looked at Alice-Miranda and shrugged.

Alice-Miranda was worried. Something was upsetting her friend and she was determined to find out exactly what it was.

☆

Jacinta walked through the back door of Grimthorpe House and almost bumped into Mrs Howard.

'Oh, thank heavens.' The old woman enveloped the child, who practically disappeared under Howie's ample frame. When she released Jacinta, the child recoiled like a spring.

Alice-Miranda and Millie arrived just behind her.

'I'm going to bed,' Jacinta mumbled, then began to walk towards the hallway.

'Oh no you don't, young lady. You are going to tell me where you've been. I was just about to call the police and your mother. You can imagine how pleased she would have been to have a third missing person on her hands in one day.'

Jacinta's face fell and she studied the floorboards.

'Well?' Mrs Howard demanded.

'Do you think you should call Mr Charles first?' asked Alice-Miranda.

'Yes, of course,' Mrs Howard replied.

Jacinta began to edge towards the door.

Howie dialled the number and turned around. She didn't notice that Jacinta had disappeared.

Charlie Weatherly was relieved that the girl had been found. He didn't ask for any further details and at that stage Mrs Howard couldn't have given them to him anyway.

She rang off and turned back to face Jacinta.

'What? Where's she gone?' Mrs Howard blustered.

'I think she went to her room,' Millie said.

'But I told her to stay right there!' Mrs Howard scratched at the creeping red rash that had made its way up her neck to her ears. The poor woman was prone to hives, particularly when she was anxious.

'We found her in the flat above the stables,' Alice-Miranda explained. 'She was asleep in the bedroom.'

'The stables?' Mrs Howard was as shocked as anyone to learn that Jacinta had gone there. 'But why?'

Alice-Miranda shook her head. 'She wouldn't say.'

'She's gone weird,' said Millie.

'Weird?' Mrs Howard repeated.

'Like when she used to throw all those tantrums, except that instead of kicking and screaming, this time she just won't talk at all. It's weird,' explained Millie.

'Yes well, thank you, Dr Millicent.' Mrs Howard scratched at her ear again. 'Perhaps it's best I talk to her in the morning. Thank you for your help, you two. Now off to bed. I'll be there in five minutes to turn off the lights.'

'I'm just glad that we found her,' Alice-Miranda said. 'She gave us an awful fright.'

Millie rolled her eyes. 'No, she didn't.'

'Well, she won't be doing it again,' Mrs Howard said. 'Not after Miss Grimm has a word to her.'

'Do you really have to tell Miss Grimm?' Alice-Miranda asked, not wanting Jacinta to get into too much trouble. She'd been hoping to talk to the headmistress herself earlier in the day but Miss Grimm and Mr Grump had been away visiting friends and hadn't been due back until late that night.

'I'm afraid I must. We can't have students running off like that, Alice-Miranda. Heavens, the girl's just about to go to high school. If she can't behave herself then perhaps she's not ready to go at all.'

Hidden from sight in the doorway of another room, Jacinta had been listening to every word. She smiled to herself and shot off down the hallway, just before Millie and Alice-Miranda headed to their rooms.

Chapter 12

Alice-Miranda was awake much earlier than she should have been, considering how late she and Millie had got to bed. She rolled over to see Millie was still fast asleep. Alice-Miranda threw off the covers and silently gathered up some clean underwear, her jodhpurs and a t-shirt. She grabbed the towel hanging on the back of the door and headed to the shower.

The room was already a hive of activity with the older girls getting ready for their orientation day at Sainsbury Palace.

'Good morning, Susannah,' Alice-Miranda said to the girl who was brushing her hair in front of the mirror.

'Hello Alice-Miranda,' Susannah smiled. 'I wish I could come out on Buttercup and help you look for Mr Parker today. I don't know why we had to have orientation day on the weekend. It's not fair!'

'I'm so sad that you're leaving,' Alice-Miranda replied. 'It won't be the same without you here and I know Bony will miss Buttercup, even though he's not always the best mannered around her.'

'I don't want to go either. None of us do. If you'd asked me a year ago, I would have said that I couldn't wait to get out of this place, but we've had so much fun lately. Miss Grimm is brilliant and Miss Reedy's English classes are amazing.'

Alice-Miranda frowned.

'What's the matter?' Susannah asked.

'Oh, nothing. I was just thinking about something you said.'

'Well, I hope you find Mr Parker,' said Susannah.

'Me too,' the tiny child called after her. 'Have a good day.'

Alice-Miranda was showered and dressed by the time Jacinta appeared in the bathroom.

'Hello,' Alice-Miranda said. 'Did you sleep well? I had lots of dreams about Mr Parker and Mrs Parker and your mother too.'

Jacinta ignored Alice-Miranda and walked straight over to one of the shower cubicles. She hung a lemon-coloured dress on the hook outside.

Alice-Miranda looked at the pretty outfit. 'I thought you had to wear your uniform for the orientation.'

'I'm not going,' Jacinta informed her.

'Why not?'

'Because I'll be grounded for sure,' Jacinta said matter-of-factly.

'Oh, Miss Grimm won't do that,' Alice-Miranda replied. 'She won't want you to miss out. You might have some extra chores to do later but I'm sure she knows how important it is for you to go to the orientation.'

Jacinta hopped into the cubicle and slammed the door.

Alice-Miranda wondered if she should go and see Miss Grimm before Mrs Howard could tell her about Jacinta's late-night expedition.

'See you at breakfast, Jacinta,' Alice-Miranda called over the noise of the shower.

There was no answer. Clearly Jacinta was upset at having done something to jeopardise her good record, thought Alice-Miranda. She knew exactly what she had to do.

☆

'Good morning, Miss Grimm,' Alice-Miranda said.

'To what do I owe this early visit?' Miss Grimm was standing in the back doorway of the flat that was part of Winchesterfield Manor. She was still in her pale pink dressing-gown, with a matching pair of fluffy slippers on her feet.

'I'm sorry to be a bother, but I really need to speak to you.'

'This sounds serious,' Miss Grimm replied.

'I think it is,' Alice-Miranda nodded. 'It's about Jacinta . . .'

Alice-Miranda was welcomed into the kitchen, where Mr Grump was sitting at the table reading the newspaper. She sat down and began to explain.

A little while later when Alice-Miranda arrived in the dining room, Jacinta was already lined up at the bain-marie, which was loaded with scrambled eggs, bacon and hash browns. Alice-Miranda slotted in behind her friend and was about to let her know about her conversation with Miss Grimm, when Miss Reedy appeared.

'Jacinta, can you tell me what you're wearing?' she asked, glaring at Jacinta's lemon-yellow dress.

'A dress,' the child said curtly.

Miss Reedy frowned. 'Of course I can see that it's a dress but it's not the right dress, is it?'

'I'm not going,' Jacinta said as she continued along the line. She dumped an extra-large spoonful of Mrs Smith's creamy scrambled eggs onto her plate.

'Of course you are,' Miss Reedy said. 'Last time I looked you were in the sixth grade.'

'But I'm in trouble. I'm sure that Miss Grimm is about to send for me at any minute and so I'm not going,' Jacinta said.

Alice-Miranda interrupted the pair. 'Excuse me, Miss Reedy, Jacinta. Good news – Miss Grimm said that of course you can go to the orientation today but she'll speak to you when you get back this evening.'

'What did you do?' Jacinta demanded.

'I knew you were upset about what happened last night and so I talked with Mrs Howard and Miss Grimm and they decided that there must have been a reason for your disappearing like that and of course it's very important that you go today so that you'll know more about the new school,' Alice-Miranda prattled.

'Disappearing?' Miss Reedy looked at Jacinta.

'It's all right, Miss Reedy. Millie and I found her and there was no harm done,' Alice-Miranda smiled.

'Really? Is that what you think?' Jacinta snatched up a slice of toast.

'It sounds to me, Jacinta, like you have Alice-Miranda to thank for not being basted today. Hurry up and eat your breakfast and I'll see you, in uniform, at the bus in twenty minutes.' Miss Reedy watched as Jacinta stalked off to a table in the far corner of the room.

Alice-Miranda looked at her teacher. 'I was only trying to help.'

'Yes, I know you were, sweetheart. Perhaps Jacinta's just going through a phase,' Miss Reedy explained.

'That's what Mummy said. I hope so. She seems awfully cross.' Alice-Miranda picked up a plate and served herself breakfast. She spotted Jacinta dumping most of her breakfast in the bin. Moments later the girl was gone.

Chapter 13

Millie had entered the dining room just as Jacinta was leaving. She told Alice-Miranda that her attempt to say hello had been completely ignored and Jacinta's face was darker than a thundercloud.

The girls decided that they would try to talk to her again that evening. There had to be a reason for her foul mood. They finished their breakfast and headed off to see Mrs Smith.

'Good morning, my lovelies,' Doreen Smith greeted the girls. 'And what can I do for you today?'

'We're going to the police station to see if we can help Constable Derby look for Mr Parker,' Alice-Miranda explained.

'We should be able to cover a fair bit of ground on Chops and Bony,' Millie added.

'And you're after some lunch to take with you, I presume.' Mrs Smith walked to the refrigerator and pulled out a slab of cold roast beef, some lettuce, tomatoes and cheese.

Both girls nodded.

'Why don't you go back to the house, brush your teeth and gather your things, and then you can pop back in ten minutes and I'll have it ready,' the cook promised. 'I do hope that they find the poor man. I've been feeling sick about it all night.'

Just as the girls were about to leave, the screen door opened and Charlie Weatherly walked in.

'Dor, are you here?' he called. The trio were in the far corner hidden by a rack of saucepans hanging above one of the giant cookers.

'Yes, Charlie,' Mrs Smith called back.

The old man walked into view. 'Morning, girls,' he nodded.

'We're going to look for Mr Parker,' Alice-Miranda informed him.

Charlie's brow knotted. 'I'm afraid that won't be necessary.'

'Has Mr Parker been found? Is he all right?' Alice-Miranda babbled.

'We don't know, but the police have found Nurse Raylene's car at one of the main train stations up north. A bag of Reg's clothes was in the boot and his watch was in the car too.'

Alice-Miranda and Millie looked at each other, then back at the adults.

'Oh.' Alice-Miranda's face fell.

'Well, at least they should be able to see whether he was with her,' Millie began. 'Don't they have cameras all over the railways?'

'Yes, they're hoping to find something, but the ticket seller said that he remembered a woman fitting Nurse Raylene's description buying two tickets and there was a man with her,' Charlie explained.

'So they should be able to find out where they've gone,' Alice-Miranda said. 'I suppose it's good news in a way. At least Mr Parker is alive and hopefully there's a good explanation for why he's gone with Nurse Raylene.'

'Can you imagine how smug Sloane will be when she hears this? She'll think she's the next Sherlock Holmes,' said Millie, rolling her eyes.

Alice-Miranda nodded. 'And poor Mrs Parker. She'll be devastated.'

'Don't you worry about Myrtle,' Mrs Smith told the girls. 'I'll bake her something nice and go and have a cup of tea with her.'

'And I'll pop over and offer to mow the lawn.' Charlie winked. 'That should help.'

'Now what about that ride?' Mrs Smith asked.

'Do you still want to go out?' Millie asked Alice-Miranda.

Alice-Miranda nodded. 'Why not? We can go exploring and then we can see Miss Hephzibah and Miss Henrietta on the way back.'

'I wonder if they know about Mr Parker,' said Millie.

'I suspect Myrtle might want to keep this news to herself for a while, now that it looks like he's run off with his nurse,' Charlie said.

'I don't suppose anyone could blame her, if that's really what's happened,' Millie said.

Alice-Miranda frowned. 'We still don't know for sure. There has to be a reason Mr Parker's gone with Nurse Raylene.'

'Because she didn't nag him to death,' Millie said with a snort.

Charlie Weatherly smiled.

'Mrs Parker's not that bad,' Alice-Miranda insisted.

Millie and Charlie exchanged grins.

'We don't have to live with her,' Millie said.

'Oh, stop that, you two,' Mrs Smith admonished. 'Now run along and get your things. I'll have your lunch ready soon and I'll call Miss Hephzibah and let her know to expect you later on.'

The girls bade the adults farewell and scampered out the back door.

Chapter 14

Silas Wiley had hoped to undertake the first part of his special mission for Finley Spencer on Saturday, but a series of disasters had put paid to that idea. For several years, Silas had run a small pizza restaurant. He'd had modest success until a well-known pizza chain had opened a shop on the high street and drawn many of his customers away. Now, just as things had finally begun to look up, the excellent young chef he'd employed had called it quits without giving any notice at all. Apparently the man had been offered twice as much money by the chain restaurant down the road. Silas hadn't a hope of matching the offer and could hardly leave the spotty fifteen-year-old assistants in charge. So he had spent his entire Saturday up to his elbows in pepperoni and cheese and wondering where he would find another chef with half the skills of his former lad.

Silas rolled over and glanced at the clock. He rubbed his eyes and was shocked to see that it was already past ten. He hopped out of bed and got under the shower. The icy water prickled his skin and he cursed the hot water heater being on the blink again.

Silas lived in the same terrace house he had grown up in. Since his parents passed away he'd been meaning to renovate but hadn't yet got around to it. Florence and Eb Wiley had not been wealthy but they had always worked hard and saved their money. Hence Silas, their only child, had been left the house and a good deal of cash. Sadly, he'd invested that in a range of faltering businesses, including the pizza restaurant and a hire-boat venture on the edge of the village. Unfortunately, a long list of new safety regulations had brought the boat business unstuck faster than a faulty zipper. These days there really wasn't any money left to buy hot water heaters or new appliances, at least not until his businesses were back in the black.

He shivered as he towelled himself dry. Silas chose a white shirt and black trousers from his immaculate wardrobe. Although the house was old and unfashionably decorated, his mother and father had taught him the virtues of being clean and tidy. His clothes were always neatly pressed and he took great pride in his appearance.

Silas finished getting dressed and headed downstairs, where he made a cup of tea and devoured some toast and jam. He opened the envelope from Finley Spencer and unfolded the map. Silas traced the road with his forefinger and wondered how long it would take to reach his destination. He'd never been to that part of the district before and hoped that his horrible sense of direction wouldn't make the assignment more difficult than it should be. If the owner hadn't responded to any of Finley's approaches, Silas wondered why she thought he'd have any more luck. But then again, he was the mayor and that carried quite some weight. Finley Spencer did say that there were rich rewards in her industry and Silas could be very persuasive when he needed to be.

Silas stacked his teacup and saucer on top of the plate and deposited them in the empty sink. He looked at the photograph of his mother and father on the sideboard and silently apologised to them for leaving the place in a mess. The washing up would have to wait.

Silas folded the map, picked up his wallet and car keys, and gathered up the envelope too. His shiny black hatchback was parked on the street out the front of the house. He hopped in and punched the destination into the satellite navigation system he'd recently had installed, courtesy of his mayoral allowance. It wasn't a good look for a man in his position to arrive late, and given that his sense of direction was more like that of a lost sheep than a homing pigeon, it was an essential piece of equipment. A route appeared and Silas started the car, eager to be on his way.

Mrs Potts was tending to her roses in the little front garden across the street. The old woman smiled and waved as Silas eased the car away from the kerb. She'd liked him since he was a little boy. That was the thing, really. Silas was a terribly likeable fellow, in spite of himself.

He turned into the high street and followed the road to the edge of the town, towards Winchesterfield. His navigation system worked a charm, although he did get rather sick of the woman inside bossing him about. Sometimes, on short journeys where he was fairly certain of the way, he'd take a deliberate wrong turn along an alternative route just so he could argue the point with her.

The little car whizzed past the turn-off to Chesterfield Downs and then the girls' school on the right and into the village. He continued past the few shops and the boys' school, Fayle, which he'd begged his parents to let him attend. Unfortunately for Silas, there was no way they could afford the fees. After he failed the scholarship examination it was totally out of the question, so instead he went to the local secondary school in Downsfordvale.

When Silas reached the turn-off he was feeling quite pleased with himself. Not one foot wrong so far. But his smug smile didn't last long. He soon found himself at the mercy of the woman inside his machine. She seemed to have as much idea about where to go as he did. He took the first turn off the main road and ended up on a narrow lane bordered on either side by low stone walls. He wondered how long it would be until he came across a sign, but the road seemed to go on forever until another lane branched off to the left. The map on the satellite navigation looked nothing like where he was. Silas had no idea which way to go so he stayed on the main track. It was no wonder Finley Spencer's people were having trouble making contact with this person. Christopher Columbus could get lost out here.

Silas was relieved when a large set of gates hove into view. At least there must be a house somewhere, he thought to himself. He turned into the driveway, past what looked to be an enormous, dilapidated stable block and on through another set of more elaborate iron gates. The overhanging trees thinned out and he found himself in the most beautiful garden. Up ahead stood one of the most magnificent mansions he'd ever seen. He couldn't understand why he'd never heard of this place before, let alone why the council didn't have it registered as part of their rather profitable open garden scheme. He'd have to talk to the owners about that.

The hatchback puttered around the carriage loop and came to a stop underneath the huge portico. The double front doors had recently been painted and the whole place had an air of renovation about it. Surely in a house this size there would be someone who could assist him with his enquiries and help him on his way.

He hopped out of the car, walked to the front doors and pressed the buzzer on the side. Chimes reverberated inside the house. Silas stood and waited for quite some time before he pressed the buzzer again. Finally the door opened and an old woman peered out.

'Hello, may I help you?' she asked.

'Yes, yes, I hope so. My name is Silas Wiley. But then again I'm sure you know that already.' He smiled broadly at her.

The woman looked blank and shook her head.

He assumed that she must be hard of hearing and repeated his name for her benefit. 'I said that I'm Silas Wiley.'

She shook her head again.

'The Mayor of Downsfordvale,' he prompted, expecting a flicker of recognition.

'That's nice, dear,' she said. 'Would you like to come in?'

What Silas really wanted was to find out where he was and get on his way, but the house was calling to him. He'd always been fascinated by great big piles like this one, and particularly how people ever had the opportunity to live in them – let alone afford their upkeep. He nodded.

'Through here,' she said and shuffled away.

Silas looked around at the beautiful entrance foyer with its dual staircases rising up either side. The woman led him through a hall that opened into a large country kitchen and directed him to sit down at the table.

'Would you like a cup of tea?'

Silas thought about it for a moment.

'It's not a trick question, dear.' She turned and filled the kettle. 'I'm having one, so it's no bother.'

Silas accepted her offer.

'I'm afraid you didn't tell me your name earlier,' he said. His eyes darted about the place, taking it all in.

'Oh, no I didn't.' She smiled. 'It's Henrietta Sykes.'

'It's lovely to meet you, Mrs Sykes, and I must say that you have a most magnificent home,' he said sincerely.

'Yes, she is a lovely old girl. A bit big though.'

'Surely you don't live here on your own?' he enquired.

'Oh no. My sister Hephzibah is here and soon

enough we're going to have a whole lot of young people too.'

He wondered what she meant. A vague memory scratched at the back of his mind. He remembered there being some debate at the council over a large house on the edge of the woods – now what were they intending to do with it again?

'Half of the house is being turned over for use as a teaching college,' Henrietta explained. 'If we can ever get the permissions through the council.' She winked at Silas.

'Oh, of course, this is Caledonia Manor, isn't it?' Silas had seen the sign on the gate and wondered why the name sounded familiar.

'Yes, we're hoping to open very soon. It will be lovely to have a house full of youngsters.'

Henrietta set a teacup down in front of Silas and offered him some milk. He nodded and she poured in rather more than he would usually have. He looked longingly at the sugar bowl but shook his head when she held it towards him.

Henrietta sat down opposite him. 'Now, how can I help you, Mr Wiley?'

'I was out here looking for someone and I fear I'm a little bit lost,' he began.

Chapter 15

Millie and Alice-Miranda returned to the kitchen to get their lunch, then walked up to the stables. Elsa had the day off and with the older students over at Sainsbury Palace for their orientation, it was very quiet.

The girls saddled Bony and Chops then wrote a note on the whiteboard outlining the time and a rough plan of where they intended to go. Alice-Miranda stood on an upturned crate and climbed into the saddle. Millie hoisted herself onto Chops's back and together they headed out into the bright sunshine.

'Do you really think that Mr Parker has gone with Nurse Raylene?' Alice-Miranda asked Millie as they walked side by side.

'Charlie seemed to think so. I can't imagine what it must be like when someone you think you know just disappears. Like the people you sometimes see on the noticeboards in the grocery shops or on breakfast cereal boxes.'

'We do that at Kennington's,' said Alice-Miranda.

'Could your father put Mr Parker on a cereal box or on some posters in the supermarkets?' Millie said.

'Oh, that's a wonderful idea. But we'd have to ask Mrs Parker's permission. She might think that it's too painful. There's a Kennington's in Downsfordvale – imagine if she shopped there and saw Mr Parker. She might get terribly upset,' said Alice-Miranda thoughtfully.

'It wouldn't hurt to ask,' Millie said.

Alice-Miranda nodded in agreement. She clicked her tongue and Bonaparte began to trot. 'Maybe we could go and see her later on. If she agrees, I'll talk to Daddy tomorrow.'

'Where do you want to go first?' Millie called as she dug her heels into Chops's flank and he caught up to his friend. Bonaparte turned around and tried to take a nip out of the little pony's ear.

'Stop that, you naughty brute.' Alice-Miranda tugged sharply at the reins. 'What if we explore the woods along the ridge? I've never been up there on Bony – only on foot when I had to do the camp at the beginning of the year. There's a pretty lookout where you can see the whole school and the village too.'

'Sounds good,' Millie replied. 'There are some secret hiding spots up there, you know. But of course, that's where you found Mr Grump.'

'He wasn't really hiding, Millie, at least not from me. But let's go and see what we can find anyway.'

Alice-Miranda ducked under a low branch. The track narrowed and she and Bony led the way as the path began to curve upwards into the side of the hill. It was quite a distance before they reached the top.

Alice-Miranda slipped down out of the saddle and took the reins over Bony's head. Millie did the same. The two girls hitched the ponies to some tree branches and walked towards a clearing.

Spread out below them was the school and the village beyond.

'Isn't it lovely?' Alice-Miranda's eyes shone as she took it all in.

'I'll say.' Millie walked around further to see if there was another vantage point. 'Come and look at this. I think you can see Caledonia Manor through the treetops.'

Alice-Miranda scurried over to her friend.

'Yes, that's the roof line.'

The woods stood between the school and Caledonia Manor. Around further was Gertrude's Grove, where the girls had met Fern and her brother Tarquin and the children from the carnival a couple of months before.

'Who owns the woods and Gertrude's Grove?' Alice-Miranda wondered out loud.

Millie shrugged. 'I'm not sure. Why do you want to know?'

'Just curious.'

'I'm starving,' announced Millie. She walked back to the ponies and opened her leather saddlebag. She retrieved two slices of devil's food cake and handed one to Alice-Miranda, who pulled out two water bottles from her own saddlebag.

Millie sat on a rock and began to unwrap her cake. Alice-Miranda sipped some water and sat beside her. She stared into the distance, wondering what she could do to help Mrs Parker. The woman seemed to like having company when she was doing the housework. Maybe Alice-Miranda could go and visit her.

A breath of wind sprung up on the ridge and Bonaparte whinnied and turned his head to look at the girls.

'No way, fat boy, you're not getting any of this cake,' Millie said with her mouth half-full.

Alice-Miranda was about to eat hers too when something caught her attention. A branch swayed lazily in front of the rock face, back and forth like a metronome. She put her cake and drink bottle down and stood up.

'Don't you want it?' Millie asked.

'I thought I saw something.' Alice-Miranda walked towards the branch.

Millie scooped up Alice-Miranda's cake just as a small trail of ants were about to enjoy a feast. She wrapped it up and scampered over to her friend.

'Millie, can you see that?'

Millie wondered what she was meant to be seeing. 'Trees?'

'No. I think there's a hole in the rock face.'

'A hole?' Millie frowned. She'd never heard anyone mention that there were caves on the ridge.

'Maybe.' Alice-Miranda dashed towards the trees and pushed the branches apart.

Sure enough, in front of them was a small hollow gouged out of the rock. It was about the size of a large dog door.

'Come on,' Alice-Miranda said.

Millie looked at her friend. 'You're not serious. You don't really want to go in there, do you?'

Alice-Miranda nodded. 'It can't hurt to poke our heads inside and take a quick look.'

'But caves can be dangerous. And there might be bats and spiders,' Millie protested.

'It can't be that bad,' Alice-Miranda reasoned.

Millie gulped. 'But we haven't got a torch.'

Alice-Miranda's face fell. 'Oh, good point.' Then her eyes lit up. 'Yes, I have. It's in my saddlebag. I put it in there a few weeks ago, just in case we were late getting back.'

'Great.' Millie tried to sound enthusiastic but she wasn't at all keen. 'You should eat this first. It might be your last meal.' She handed Alice-Miranda her slightly squashed piece of cake.

Alice-Miranda giggled. 'Thanks, I'll save it for later. You're not turning into Sloane, are you?' She put the back of her hand against her forehead dramatically.

'What? Oh, a drama queen. No, of course not!'

Alice-Miranda shot off back to the ponies and rummaged about in the bottom of her saddlebag. She found the little torch just where she'd put it, then shoved the cake inside and raced back to where Millie was peering into the darkness.

'It's not a very big gap.' Millie wondered how tight it would be once they were inside.

'It's just as well we're both small then.' Alice-Miranda knelt down and held the torch in her teeth. She shone the light and wriggled through the opening.

'Can you see anything?' Millie stood outside, hoping that the cavity led straight into another rock wall.

There was a mumbling noise and then silence.

'Are you all right in there?' Millie called. She wondered why Alice-Miranda had gone quiet.

There was another long pause.

'Come on, that's not funny,' Millie said. 'Are you okay? I was just kidding before about your last meal, Alice-Miranda.'

There was a thud from inside as Alice-Miranda dropped the torch from her mouth and stood up. She brushed the dirt off her jodhpurs and retrieved the light from the ground.

'Wow! Millie, you should see this.' Her words echoed. 'It's a proper cave. It's not huge but I can stand up. Come on!'

'Is it safe?' Millie called back, relieved to hear Alice-Miranda's voice.

'I think so. We won't go far. But you have to see it. It's so pretty.'

Millie turned and looked at Chops and Bonaparte. 'If we're not back in half an hour, make a lot of noise, will you, or go and look for someone if you can untie yourselves.' She was only half-joking.

Bonaparte whinnied and shook his head up and down in reply, as if he'd understood perfectly.

Millie knelt down and pushed herself through the little opening. It was longer than she'd anticipated, a bit like a rocky cocoon. She could see the light from Alice-Miranda's torch in the distance.

'Oh my goodness,' Millie gasped as her head popped out on the other side. She stood up. 'I didn't expect this.'

Chapter 16

Bonaparte and Chops cantered through the woods on their way to Caledonia Manor. Alice-Miranda and Millie wondered if anyone else knew about the cave. They couldn't wait to tell Miss Hephzibah and Miss Henrietta about their discovery.

Alice-Miranda caught sight of someone digging in the pretty garden near the fountain. 'Miss Hephzibah,' she called.

Hepzibah Fayle wiped her brow and used her special garden kneeling frame to help her stand up.

'Hello girls, it's lovely to see you both.'

'We've got some amazing news,' Millie yelled.

'Ride up to the house and I'll meet you there in a minute,' Hephzibah instructed. 'I think I've had enough weeding for one day.' She gathered her little digger and the kneeling frame and headed towards the house.

Alice-Miranda and Millie noticed a little black car parked under the portico. Each girl wondered who it belonged to, although with the teaching college due to open soon, there seemed to be people coming and going all the time.

The girls rode their ponies to the rear of the house, let them have a drink at the old trough near the back flowerbeds, and tied them to the balustrades on the lower lawn. Miss Hephzibah was making her way along the veranda towards the kitchen door and was almost bowled over as the children ran to greet her.

'Hello,' cried Alice-Miranda as she launched herself around Hephzibah's waist.

'Well, hello to you too.' Hephzibah bent down and kissed the top of Alice-Miranda's head. She took a step back and looked at the child. 'Are you all right, dear?'

Alice-Miranda gazed up into the old woman's blue eyes. She nodded. 'Yes, of course. It's just been a strange couple of days.'

'Why don't you come inside and tell me all about it over a nice cold glass of lemonade.' Hephzibah turned to give Millie a hug too and together they entered the kitchen.

Henrietta Sykes was sitting at the scrubbed pine table with a book open in front of her. Her reading glasses were balanced on the tip of her nose and she almost leapt out of her seat when the screen door banged shut.

'Oh, girls,' she gasped. 'I was deep in thought. Wonderful story this.' She waved the book around. It fell with a thump back onto the table.

'Asleep, did you say, Henny?' her sister teased.

'No, no, I wasn't sleeping. Reading, that's what I was doing.'

'Who owns the black car at the front door?' her sister asked.

'Oh, it belongs to a lovely man. Mr Wiley,' Henrietta replied.

Hephzibah looked around the kitchen. 'Have you hidden him in a cupboard, dear?'

Alice-Miranda and Millie giggled, then pecked

Henrietta on both cheeks before walking to the sink to wash their hands.

'Of course not. He's just gone to the toilet. He was very keen to have a look around the house and you know I can't really manage the stairs, so I told him to take a little tour upstairs as well.'

Hephzibah nodded, and then noticed the girls' grubby knees and elbows. 'Where have you two been? You don't usually get quite that dirty when you're riding.'

'Exploring,' said Alice-Miranda excitedly.

'Exploring?' Hephzibah repeated. 'That sounds intriguing.'

Meanwhile upstairs, Silas Wiley had given himself a grand tour of Caledonia Manor. He thought the ladies had made a very good use of the space. The bedrooms had been converted into classrooms as well as an accommodation wing. He rather fancied living there himself – it was certainly much more modern than his own home. As he made his way back to the kitchen, he could hear voices. He presumed that Mrs Sykes's sister had returned from wherever she had been. Then he heard a child's voice too. He stopped in the hallway outside, not wanting to interrupt.

'We found a cave,' said the child's voice. Silas heard a chair being pulled out and the *whump* of an excited little body collapsing onto it. 'Well, Alice-Miranda found it. At the top of the ridge in the woods.'

Silas nodded. A cave? That sounded like fun. He listened more intently, imagining what it would have been like to grow up having the run of a grand estate like this with all those lovely grounds to explore.

'Well, I hope you didn't go inside,' Henrietta said seriously.

Not likely, Silas thought to himself. Any child worth their salt would definitely take a look.

'We did and it was amazing,' came another child's voice. The one called Alice-Miranda? Silas heard another chair being pulled from the table.

'And what did you find in this cave?' Henrietta asked.

Silas pressed his ear against the door. He was expecting the big discovery to be a bat or perhaps an animal skeleton.

'I'll make us a fresh pot of tea,' came another adult's voice, 'and get you girls that lemonade.'

'Gold!' one of the children exclaimed loudly.

Silas almost choked. He had to stop himself from

coughing as he crept back to the bottom of the stairs. He wondered if he'd heard correctly. Gold? Really?

In the kitchen, Henrietta glanced at the door, wondering if her visitor was about to return. She could have sworn she heard a shuffling sound in the hallway.

'Gold? Are you sure?' Hephzibah scoffed. 'I can't imagine that there's any gold in those hills.'

'Oh yes, we saw it with our own eyes,' said Alice-Miranda. 'I wondered if I was seeing things too, but I'm fairly certain that it's real.'

'The cave looked like it was covered in fairy dust and then Alice-Miranda found a long white line in the rock. It changed colour and then it became even wider and it turned into gold,' Millie gushed.

'That's a lovely story, girls. But you mustn't tell anyone,' said Henrietta carefully.

'Why not?' Millie asked. She had visions of being featured on the local news.

'Well, you don't know for certain that it is gold and if it is, can you imagine the trouble it might cause?'

Millie wondered what she was talking about. 'Trouble?'

'Do you really want people clambering all over

our lovely mountains in search of gold, tearing the cave apart and making an awful mess of the place?'

Alice-Miranda shook her head. 'I hadn't thought of that.'

'Oh, of course not,' Millie frowned.

'Gold gives men a fever, you know,' Henrietta said seriously. 'Makes them sick with greed.'

'Can we at least tell our friends?' Millie asked.

'Do you mean Jacinta and Sloane?' Hephzibah asked as she placed a steaming cup of tea in front of her sister. 'Do you think that would be wise?'

Millie thought about it. Sloane's mother was quite possibly the greediest, most conniving woman on earth and for a while it looked as if Sloane was a carbon copy. Jacinta's mother had been married to an incredibly wealthy man who had all but left her with nothing. Perhaps Miss Hephzibah was right.

'Don't you think it's a delicious secret?' Hephzibah said. 'Just between the two of you, like the secrets sisters have.'

Alice-Miranda looked at Hephzibah and then at Henrietta. 'Do you have secrets?'

'Oh yes, dear, of course we do. You can't know

someone your whole life and not have secrets,' Hephzibah replied.

Alice-Miranda thought about it. 'You know, Millie, you are just like my big sister and even though I've only known you for less than a year, by the time we're Miss Henrietta's and Miss Hephzibah's age, it will feel like we've known each other forever, just like sisters.'

'And if I had to have a little sister, I'd definitely choose you,' Millie replied, looking at her friend.

'Well, it's settled then.' Henrietta smiled at Hephzibah. 'The cave and the gold will remain a special secret between sisters.'

'Hep, dear, is there any more of that date slice?' Henrietta asked.

Silas stayed in the hallway for another minute before striding noisily into the kitchen. 'Lovely renovation, Mrs Sykes,' he announced as he walked through the door.

The girls and Hephzibah turned to look at him.

'Oh, hello, I didn't realise there was anyone else here,' Silas lied.

'Hep, this is Mr Wiley,' said Henrietta. She looked at her visitor. 'Did you get lost up there?'

He smiled widely. 'No, no, there's just so much to look at.'

Alice-Miranda approached Silas. 'Hello Mr Wiley, my name is Alice-Miranda Highton-Smith-Kennington-Jones.' She held out her hand and he shook it gently.

'Good afternoon. And actually it's Mayor Wiley.' He played her name over in his mind. Highton, Kennington. 'Your parents aren't Cecelia Highton-Smith and Hugh Kennington-Jones, are they?' he asked, realising he was possibly in the presence of retailing royalty.

'Oh, yes.' Alice-Miranda smiled. 'Do you know them?'

'I wish,' Silas muttered and then raised his voice to say, 'Oh yes, of course. Man in my position and all that.'

'This is my friend, Millicent Jane McLoughlin-McTavish-McNoughton-McGill.' Alice-Miranda gestured towards the flame-haired girl.

Millie looked over from where she was sitting. 'You can just call me Millie. Are you really the mayor?'

'Yes, that's right,' he replied.

'And to what do we owe this honour, Mr Wiley?' Hephzibah asked.

'I was on my way to see someone and got a little bit lost, but your very kind sister has given me directions. I should be on my way or I'll never get there,' Silas said as he picked up his jacket from the back of one of the kitchen chairs.

'Are you sure you wouldn't like a cup of tea? And I haven't offered anyone a bite to eat. Are you girls hungry? Would you like a sandwich?' Hephzibah stood up and walked to the small tower of biscuit tins on the bench. She prised the lid off the top one and put half a dozen chocolate coconut slices onto a pretty plate, then located some date slice, which she added to the offering.

'No, I must get going,' Silas said reluctantly. His stomach gurgled. The morning tea treats looked rather delicious.

'I'll see you out then.' Henrietta pushed herself up slowly from where she was sitting. She reached for her walking stick.

'Goodbye Major Wiley.' Alice-Miranda waved. Millie did too.

He followed Henrietta into the front hall.

'Are you sure I can't get you two something to eat?' said Hephzibah vaguely. She was wondering where exactly Mr Wiley was on his way to.

'Mrs Smith made us some lunch,' Alice-Miranda said. 'We might ride over to Gertrude's Grove later and have it there. But I'd love a piece of slice.'

Chapter 17

First thing Sunday morning, Constable Derby and a team of detectives from Downsfordvale scoured every inch of Myrtle Parker's home for clues. Myrtle had hovered over the police men and women, watching them like a hawk lest they break anything or make a mess. She really wasn't in any fit state to do housework and although Ambrosia was being particularly helpful, she felt that the woman would probably draw the line at vacuuming.

'What are you looking for here, constable?'

Myrtle asked. 'You should be at the railway station where you found that rotten woman's car.'

'I'm sure the detectives up north are there now,' Constable Derby replied.

At first he'd been perplexed about how Mr Parker would have been able to stand up after all that time in bed. But the man's doctor had explained that with all the daily exercise Nurse Raylene had been doing with Reginald, the massages and the special muscle stimulation machine that Mrs Parker had procured for his treatment, there was a good chance Reginald would be in quite sound condition – although he'd likely be a bit wobbly to begin with. The doctor said that the last time he'd been to check on Mr Parker, he'd been very impressed with the man's muscle tone; what he couldn't understand was how Reginald could suddenly regain consciousness and decide to leave with a woman he didn't know.

'I knew she was a vixen from the moment I laid eyes on her. I should never have let her get so close to my Reginald. It's just that I hardly had the time to spend every moment with him, did I? What with running the show committee and helping the Fayle sisters and visiting the sick and infirmed, I just couldn't possibly do it all. And then there were all the jobs I had to do. I mean, look at all that cleaning and gardening!'

Ambrosia Headlington-Bear heard the last comment and pursed her lips. Myrtle Parker had not pulled one weed in that front yard of hers. She wondered why she let the woman get away with saying so, but thought better than to make a scene. After all, they'd both been through difficult times and on some strange level, Ambrosia had taken great comfort in her friendship with Myrtle.

'Well, I think we're done,' Constable Derby said, after consulting with the detectives. They'd found nothing suspicious.

Myrtle Parker walked into the front sitting room, where Reginald's hospital bed sat empty. 'That's it then.' She patted the mattress. 'I'll call and have this returned to the hospital tomorrow morning, shall I?'

Constable Derby frowned. 'Oh, uh . . .'

'Are you sure you don't want to leave that a few days, Myrtle? I can arrange it for you,' Ambrosia offered.

'Why would I leave it?' Myrtle snapped. 'It's clear he's not going to need it any more.'

Constable Derby looked embarrassed. 'I'll be off then, Mrs Parker.' He walked towards the front hallway. 'I'll let you know if we hear anything more.'

But Myrtle Parker was already halfway through stripping the sheets off the bed. She didn't notice the envelope that had slipped down into the folds of the cotton blanket. She bundled the sheets and blanket together and added the pillow slip.

'Ambrosia, would you pop these into the machine for me?' she instructed. 'They can all go in together. I'll call the hospital.'

Ambrosia frowned. She'd get to it shortly, after she finished the washing up.

Constable Derby let himself out. He wondered if Myrtle Parker really would be all right.

Chapter 18

Silas Wiley's mind was racing. Gold? Had he really heard the child correctly? He sped down the driveway with the directions in his hand. Mrs Sykes had seemed fairly certain she knew the way to Wood End, although she said she hadn't visited the place in years and had no idea if anyone still lived there.

Silas made his way back to the main road, turned right and continued for a couple of miles. He slowed down, looking for another lane off to the right. Thick undergrowth had all but consumed an ancient stone wall and an unkempt hedge shielded whatever lay behind it, making it very difficult to see anything. He was quite certain that he'd gone too far when he spotted the opening to a half-covered track. Silas nudged the car into the space and realised that beyond the overhanging willow branches there was indeed a narrow lane. He pushed a little further in, hoping that if he was wrong, he'd be able to back out again.

A flash of red caught his eye. He stopped the car, reached out the window and pushed some vines aside. This revealed a dilapidated red letterbox with a faint sign: 'Wood End'.

'Well, that's a start,' Silas muttered to himself. Whoever lived at the end of the road didn't want to be easily found. He proceeded down the track, slowing over the many pits and potholes.

Silas was pleased to see that a little further along, the road opened up. As the track became smoother, he pressed his foot harder on the accelerator. The countryside around him was still quite dense but he could see a narrow timber bridge up ahead. He decided to check it before taking the car across. It was just as well that he did; when he prodded the first timber slat with his foot, it disintegrated beneath him, sending particles of dust floating into the stream below.

Silas turned and looked at the car. 'Looks like I'll be walking from here,' he murmured. He retrieved the car keys, hit the remote lock and set off on foot.

He looked up and down the waterway, hoping to find an easy way across, and was pleased to see a wide log, which looked as though it had been put there for just that purpose. Silas trod carefully, glancing into the crystal water, and was thrilled to see a large trout swimming against the current. He'd have to bring his fly rod next time. This looked to be a gem of a spot.

The distance to the house from here was anyone's guess. He thought he must have gone almost a mile when the woodland was replaced by an expanse of green. Ahead of him stood an unexpectedly pretty stone cottage. Two storeys tall, surrounded by a low stone wall and sitting among a particularly well-tended flower garden, it was most certainly someone's home.

'Well, this is a surprise,' Silas said aloud. He was hoping that if the owner kept dogs, they were chained up or friendly. He wasn't much of a dog lover himself – they'd made him nervous ever since a particularly nasty bull terrier had removed a chunk of his left buttock when he was a boy. Silas glanced at the picturesque surroundings. There were several outbuildings to the rear of the cottage and a rusty red tractor sitting in a field beyond a fence. He could hear the honking of geese and clucking of chickens. Even these made him a little nervous – geese had a reputation for being better guard dogs than the real thing.

Wherever the animals were, they didn't come to greet him. The driveway led Silas around to the rear of the property, past a bountiful vegetable patch to the back door.

'Hello,' he called and knocked at the same time. 'Is anyone here?'

There was no reply. He tried again a few minutes later but there was still no response. Silas glanced around at the outbuildings and decided to try his luck there.

A series of sheds was attached to a barn and some animal enclosures. Silas walked towards the largest of the buildings, and noticed two goats standing on the roof of a lean-to, bleating noisily. He wondered how on earth they got up there.

More of the animals had noticed the stranger in their yard. Silas called out again above a rising cacophony of barnyard sounds. 'Hello, is anyone about?' He peered through the open doorway. His eyes adjusted to the low light but he couldn't see anyone inside.

There was a rusty Cortina, its rear-vision mirror draped in cobwebs. The driver's window was down and it looked as if a bird had built a nest on the dashboard. Beyond the car, a vast workbench ran the length of the building. Unlike the vehicle, the bench was pristine. A pegboard hung above it, with each saw and pair of pliers it housed neatly outlined in thick black texta. 'A place for everything and everything in its place' – he could hear his own father saying it as he scanned the array of tools. Silas looked more closely and noticed that several things were missing. Two picks, and a couple of oval shapes. He tried to think what they might have been. A shovel was missing from its mount as well.

This assignment was proving far more difficult than he'd hoped. If he couldn't find the owner, he couldn't very well talk them into a meeting with Finley Spencer now, could he?

There was a shuffling sound behind him. 'Oh, there you are,' said Silas. He turned around and was stunned to find himself nose to nose with a donkey.

He was even more surprised when the creature started making a noise that sounded something like a crying baby with a terrible dose of the hiccups.

Silas began to laugh, which only seemed to make the animal more excited. It's strangled hee-haws grew higher and higher.

'Come along, then.' Silas reached out to push the beast away. But the donkey stood its ground.

'All right, very funny, now move to the left,' Silas commanded.

The donkey stopped its racket and leapt to the right.

Silas decided he'd head left then. But as he did, the donkey shuffled to the other side and blocked his path. He laughed.

'You want to play a game, do you?'

Silas leaned to the right and the donkey did the same. He leaned to the left and sure enough the little brown beast mirrored his actions.

'Well, you're very funny but that's quite enough. I have to find the owner of this splendid patch. I don't suppose you know where he is?' Silas was beginning to feel claustrophobic. He looked around to see if there was another way out of the shed. The donkey began to bray again, even more loudly than before.

'Stop that racket, I can't think,' Silas barked. He reached out to pat the beast, hoping it would calm down.

Snap! The donkey almost took his fingers off.

'Hey, that's not funny at all. Now let me get past, you hairy brute.'

The donkey shuffled to the other side of the passageway, like a football player trying to avoid a tackle.

Silas was growing tired of this game. 'Come on, get out of my way.'

But the donkey stood its ground, shuffling left and right and keeping Silas bailed up in the shed.

The man edged backwards to the bench at the rear of the building. He noticed that the gap between the car and the other wall wasn't very wide. Maybe he could squeeze through and make a run for it when the donkey wasn't looking.

Silas was about to give it a go when something caught his attention. It was a trunk under the bench. He knew it was none of his business and yet for some reason he wanted to see inside. The donkey seemed to have lost interest in him for the moment and was nosing about through the car window. Silas leaned down and pulled the trunk out just far enough to lift the lid.

At first he thought it contained just a pile of old notebooks but Silas reached in further and pulled out a small glass jam jar. He held it up towards the daylight, wondering who would have collected the little container of rocks. A fond memory entered his mind, of gathering seashells at the beach and keeping them in a little glass jar under his own bed as a child.

Something glinted in the half-light. He studied the jar more closely. Silas turned and looked back at the workbench. He thought for a moment, looked at the jar again and all of a sudden the missing tools made perfect sense. The child at Caledonia Manor was telling the truth. 'Oh my, Ms Spencer, have I got some news for you,' Silas muttered.

Silas slipped the jar into his jacket pocket. He pushed the chest back under the bench and looked at the donkey.

'Let's see you get me now,' Silas taunted the animal. He edged between the car and the wall. It took a few moments for the beast to realise exactly what was going on. It trotted around the back of the car and pushed its way into the narrow gap. Silas was almost through. 'Come on, my little friend,' he coaxed.

The donkey forced its way further along and just as Silas had hoped, found itself wedged between the car and the wall, its stomach stuck fast.

'That will teach you to mess with Silas Wiley, you stupid ass.' Silas pushed through and ran out of the shed. He left the little donkey hee-hawing at the top of its lungs and shuffling to reverse out of the space.

Silas glanced around the farmyard and over to where the two goats had been standing atop the lean-to. The roof was now clear. He ran past the back of the cottage, down the track and towards the stream. It was faster than he'd run in a long time. As the stream came into view, Silas slowed to a jog. He smiled to himself, thinking just how pleased Finley Spencer would be to hear from him now.

He felt for the jar and pulled it out into the sunlight. 'What on earth is this place really worth?'

Silas crossed the stream and looked up the bank towards his car.

'Hey! Get away from there!' he yelled and ran towards the vehicle. 'Stop that!'

But no amount of screaming and hand-waving was going to deter these two from their feast. Standing on the bonnet was one little goat, who was eating the windscreen wipers. The other goat had all but demolished the driver's side mirror.

Silas pressed the remote door lock and made a run for it, lunging through the passenger door and slamming it shut behind him. He wriggled across into the driver's seat and started the engine. Even that didn't frighten the horrid beasts. He slammed his hand on the dashboard.

'Get off!' Silas screeched. He blasted the horn.

'Crazy animals!' Silas spluttered as he turned the key in the ignition and shoved the car into gear, before reversing at top speed to the edge of the track. The goat on the bonnet lost its grip and slipped off the side. Fortunately it was a nimble creature and quickly found its feet. It avoided the spinning wheels as Silas planted his foot on the accelerator. Silas saw the other, mirror-eating beast tripping over the rickety remains of the bridge towards home, with a chunk of black plastic hanging out of its mouth. Silas's hatchback fishtailed along the track, the overhanging foliage slapping the car as he sped back towards the main road.

He wondered what state the vehicle would be in by the time he got home. Silas had always been a little precious about his car, but the jar in his pocket told him that a new one was on the agenda. Probably a new house and a rather nice holiday as well. But first he needed some time to think – this mission had become rather complicated. Surely Finley Spencer would be very grateful to know that Wood End was a far more valuable proposition than she'd first thought. Besides, even if the old fellow didn't want to sell, Finley could claim mining rights without his permission anyway. Silas would of course be richly rewarded for his discovery. He couldn't wait to get home and go for a run – it would help clear his head.

☆

Stan and Reg had spent another full day in the cave. As always it had proved entirely fruitless. Despite Stan's concerns about where Reg had been all this time, their friendship had taken up much as it had left off. They didn't talk a lot but it was nice to have some human company.

Stan wondered if he should send Reg home but the man seemed perfectly happy to potter about. He kept talking about his dream, which was perplexing; the cave he described was certainly not the one they were in. Stan thought the silly old fellow's mind was playing tricks but Reg was sure that with a little more searching, they'd find it.

Stan didn't share his friend's confidence but he was enjoying being back there. His days alone gardening had stretched endlessly together and given him too much time to think about a life that could almost certainly have been different, if Beryl hadn't been so stubborn. He tried not to let his mind wander to the past too often. It was easier to block things out and pretend they never existed. When Beryl told him to leave the issue alone, he'd all but given up hope of ever finding her. But now Beryl was gone and he wasn't getting any younger, Stan found himself wishing more than ever that one day she'd find her way home.

'Come on, Reg, let's call it a day,' Stan said. 'It'll still be here tomorrow.'

Reginald Parker turned towards his friend, his little round light shining into Stan's eyes.

'All right, I can barely keep my eyes open anyway. Don't know what's got into me lately.' Reg gathered his tools and walked towards the cave's hidden entrance.

'Old age, my friend. We're getting on. What are you now? Seventy?' Stan asked.

'Pffft. I'm sixty-seven next birthday,' Reg replied.

Stan did some silent calculations. He was soon to be seventy-two and he knew Reg was only two years younger.

'Well, if you're sixty-seven, then I'll happily take sixty-nine – again.' Stan shook his head.

The two men carefully made their way down the track.

Stan looked at the little brown donkey, who was standing by the gate munching on some long grass. 'Good afternoon, Cynthia. Anything interesting happen while we were away?'

Cynthia hee-hawed a greeting and went back to her grazing. Cherry and Pickles were huddled like co-conspirators further along the fence.

Stan noticed something hanging out of Cherry's mouth. 'What have you got there?' He opened the gate and was surprised to find the latch not properly fixed.

'What is that?' He peered at the goat's mouth. She began to chew more quickly. 'Come on now.' Stan reached into his pocket and found a couple of boiled sweets. He held them out and the two goats strutted towards him. Cherry dropped the black object in exchange for the barley sugar. Pickles quickly hoovered up her treat too.

Stan bent down and picked up the slimy piece of rubber.

'What is it, Stan?' Reg asked from the other side of the fence.

'Looks like . . . I don't know.' Stan walked back through the gate, fixed the latch securely, and handed the item to Reg.

He turned it over in his hands. 'Looks like part of a windscreen wiper blade, if you ask me.'

Stan frowned. He wondered where it could have come from.

'Maybe you had a visitor?' Reg suggested.

Stan shook his head. 'Couldn't get past the bridge these days. The old girl's half-collapsed into the stream.'

'One of life's mysteries then,' Reg said with a grin.

Stan frowned. There'd been a few of those lately.

Chapter 19

That afternoon, as Millie and Alice-Miranda made their way back to school, Alice-Miranda couldn't stop thinking about Mr Parker. Millie was disappointed that their amazing discovery would have to remain a secret.

'Do you really think anyone cares that much?' Millie asked as the pair trotted along on Bony and Chops.

'Of course everyone cares about Mr Parker,' Alice-Miranda replied, wondering at her friend's unfeeling remark.

'No, I didn't mean about him,' Millie scoffed. 'I meant about the gold.'

'Oh!' Alice-Miranda smiled. 'Sorry, my mind has been in a whirl about Mr Parker.'

'I'm not that mean, you know,' Millie said.

'No, of course not,' Alice-Miranda grinned.

'Well, my father always says that if there's a chance to make a fortune easily, people tend to go a bit mad,' said Alice-Miranda.

'I don't care about the money,' Millie said. 'I just thought it was exciting that we made a discovery. Like real adventurers.'

'It was exciting,' Alice-Miranda agreed. 'But we mustn't tell. We promised Miss Hephzibah and Miss Henrietta that we wouldn't.'

Millie placed her hand over her heart and pronounced loudly, 'All right then. The secret of the golden cave will go with me to my grave.'

Alice-Miranda smiled. 'You don't need to be quite so melodramatic about it, Millie. Maybe when we're older there'll be a reason to tell someone.'

'Okay,' said Millie. 'I wonder if Jacinta will be in a better mood when we get back?'

'I hope so. I can't understand what's made her so cross the past couple of days,' Alice-Miranda said.

Millie shrugged. 'Who knows? Come on, I'll race you to the stables.' She clicked her tongue and dug her heels into Chops's flank.

'Hey! Wait for me.' Alice-Miranda gave Bony a sharp kick and the little pony took off at top speed. The girls were neck and neck as they flew through the undergrowth and into the home paddock.

Millie leapt out of the saddle and tied Chops to the low rail outside the stable block before racing inside to retrieve two brushes and a couple of carrots. Alice-Miranda tied Bonaparte up beside the little bay gelding. She undid the girth strap and pulled Bony's saddle and cloth off his sweaty back.

She carried them into the tack room and returned with Bony's stall halter, which she quickly swapped for his bridle. Millie was in the process of doing the same when Susannah appeared.

'Hello,' Alice-Miranda called as she glimpsed the older girl walking up the drive.

Susannah waved and called 'hello' back.

Millie returned from the tack room and said hello too. 'How was the orientation?'

Susannah frowned. 'It was terrible. Well, *it* wasn't terrible but Jacinta was.'

Millie ducked under Chops's neck and looked at Susannah.

'You're never going to believe this . . .' the girl began.

Alice-Miranda stopped brushing Bony's tummy and looked up. Her own tummy fluttered at the thought of Jacinta being in trouble. 'What did she do?'

'Well, you know how we were going there to try some classes and have a proper look around the school?' said Susannah.

Millie nodded. She didn't really know that but she wanted Susannah to hurry up and get on with the story.

Susannah continued. 'We had a Science lesson to start with and the teacher was going to show us how to use a Bunsen burner and do an experiment.'

'That sounds interesting,' said Alice-Miranda. 'Mrs Oliver has some of those in the laboratory at Highton Hall. She showed me how they work but I'm not allowed to touch unless she's supervising. They can be very dangerous.'

Susannah nodded.

'So did you do the experiment?' Millie asked, then turned her attention back to untangling a knot in Chops's mane.

'No. The teacher was terrifying and made us all feel like idiots. When we got into the classroom he told everyone to stand up and then he went around the room asking each girl to name one of the elements on the periodic table,' Susannah explained.

Millie looked bewildered. 'What's that?'

'Exactly,' said Susannah. 'I only know what it is because my dad's a chemist. Mr Plumpton was there and he tried to explain that we hadn't covered the topic this year. But Professor Crookston – that's the scary teacher – snapped and asked if Mr Plumpton taught Science or Needlework. Poor Mr Plumpton's nose was glowing like Rudolph's and we all thought he might cry.'

'That's awful. Then what happened?' Alice-Miranda asked as she brushed Bonaparte's flank.

'Well, Professor Crookston went around the room and kept staring at each girl until she said something. Fortunately he looked at me first and then Ashima, whose mum's a scientist, and so we started them off and some of the girls made good guesses. But then he got to Jacinta and it all went downhill.'

'Why? What did she do?' Millie asked.

'She didn't say anything for ages. And he just kept staring at her.'

'What does he look like?' Alice-Miranda asked.

'Dangerous. He has jet-black hair, all shiny like a crow, and he can make one eyebrow go up and the other go down at the same time.'

'So what happened next?' Millie asked.

Susannah looked as if she could hardly bear to speak of it. 'Professor Crookston asked Jacinta to go to the front of the room and then he roared at her and said that he'd never met such a stupid imbecile in all his life.'

Alice-Miranda gasped. 'Poor Jacinta, that's awful! She's hasn't been herself lately anyway, so this must have finished her off.' She felt sick for her friend.

'Not exactly,' said Susannah. 'You should have seen her. She was amazing. She didn't flinch, not even when he was yelling right in her face. She just stared at him as if she'd gone into a trance.'

'Teachers can't yell at children like that. It's not right,' Millie declared.

'Try telling Professor Crookston that,' said Susannah.

'What did Mr Plumpton do?' Alice-Miranda asked.

'He walked over to Professor Crookston and asked him to calm down, but that only made him yell more. It was lucky that they were distracted for a moment. I mouthed "gold" to Jacinta, and pointed at my finger as if I were wearing a ring. She said it out loud but they didn't hear her and then she shouted "gold" and Professor Crookston stopped. He glared at her and said, "So you're not as stupid as you look." Jacinta just walked back to where she was sitting without a word. We all thought she was terribly brave.'

'What happened then?'

'The professor called her back again and said that as she was so clever she could demonstrate how to use a Bunsen burner. Mr Plumpton told him that we had no experience but he insisted that Jacinta would be all right. So he handed her a box of matches and said that she should show everyone how to light the contraption.'

'That sounds dangerous,' said Alice-Miranda, frowning. 'The Bunsen burners in Mrs Oliver's laboratory are all hooked up to the gas and I know even she has trouble lighting them sometimes.'

'So what happened? Did she do it?' Millie asked.

'She struck a few matches before getting one to burn. By then you could smell the gas. Then she lit the flame and turned the little dial and it seemed to be going well. Professor Crookston said that perhaps she'd get through Science after all.'

Alice-Miranda let out a breath. 'Well, that's a relief.'

'Not really. The professor had a pile of worksheets on the bench and Jacinta accidentally knocked the Bunsen burner over when she was trying to move it. The papers erupted into flames and the whole front bench caught alight. Mr Plumpton raced to get the fire blanket. Danika grabbed a bucket from the sink near where she was sitting and just as Mr Plumpton threw the blanket over the fire, Danika threw the bucket of water. The fire was out but Professor Crookston was soaked. Jacinta, Danika and Mr Plumpton were all standing there with their mouths open and then Professor Crookston let out this sound like, I don't know, like nothing I've ever heard before – maybe a wounded elephant.'

Susannah shook her head in amazement before continuing. 'He roared at Jacinta and said that she'd done it on purpose just to make him look bad. You can imagine how Jacinta reacted. We could see her getting madder and madder and then she exploded too, telling him that he was the meanest teacher she'd ever met and she wouldn't want to be in his stupid Science class anyway, and how dare he embarrass the girls by asking them things they had never learned before.'

'Oh my goodness, that's terrible. What happened next?' Alice-Miranda's face was pale.

'He grabbed Jacinta by the collar and dragged her out of the room. Poor Mr Plumpton was spluttering and frothing and calling out that it was an accident and he needed to let go of her. Professor Crookston just yelled that Mr Plumpton had to watch the rest of the "feral children" and he would deal with her as he should have done in the first place.'

'Where is she now?' Alice-Miranda asked.

'We don't know,' Susannah said.

Millie gawked at her. 'What do you mean you don't know?'

'We finished our lessons and had lunch, which was disgusting, and then there were some games afterwards on the field with another cranky teacher and we got to have a look through the boarding house too, but Jacinta didn't come back.'

'What did Miss Reedy and Mr Plumpton say? Surely they knew where she was?' said Alice-Miranda.

'They just said that Jacinta wouldn't be coming

back to school until later and that her mother would have to go and pick her up.'

'Poor Jacinta,' Alice-Miranda said.

Susannah nodded. 'I know. I heard some of the other girls whispering that although Mrs Jelly, the headmistress, might look soft and wobbly, underneath she makes the old Miss Grimm look like Glinda, the Good Witch of the South. You know, the Miss Grimm you met when you first arrived, Alice-Miranda.'

'That sounds bad,' Alice-Miranda said. 'And if Mrs Jelly has teachers like Professor Crookston in the school, that could well be true.'

'Jacinta might get expelled,' Millie said.

'Can she be expelled before she's actually started?' Susannah asked.

'I don't think so. But they could revoke her entrance,' Alice-Miranda reasoned, 'although I imagine the school would love to have someone with her gymnastics ability, given their reputation.'

Susannah nodded. 'I hope so. Now, I'd better get moving. I only have time to give Buttercup a quick brush. Miss Reedy told us we had to be back at the dining room for afternoon tea so we could have a debriefing about the day.'

'Gosh, is it that time already?' Alice-Miranda turned and looked at the clock that hung on the far wall.

'You don't have to come down though,' Susannah said.

'No, but I'm starving.' Millie's tummy grumbled on cue. She was also dying to find out what had happened to Jacinta.

'Where did you go today?' Susannah asked as she opened the door to Buttercup's stable and walked inside.

'Up on the ridge,' Alice-Miranda said.

'But there was nothing at all interesting up there,' Millie added.

Alice-Miranda shot her friend a warning look.

'Then we went to Miss Hephzibah's and to Gertrude's Grove, where we had a picnic and played some games near the creek,' Alice-Miranda finished.

'I'm going to miss being here so much,' Susannah said. 'I love riding with you two and I don't even know if I'll be able to take Buttercup to Sainsbury Palace because they're doing some renovations on the stable block and talking about turning it into an art studio. I can't imagine not having her with me.' Buttercup nickered softly as if to agree. 'And

I'm scared about the teachers. I don't want to go at all any more.'

'School should be fun,' Alice-Miranda declared. 'If it's fun then it's much easier to learn.'

Alice-Miranda finished rubbing Bonaparte down before swapping her brush for a hoof pick. Millie led Chops into his stable and organised his dinner. Soon Alice-Miranda did the same.

'There you go, boy.' Alice-Miranda added a handful of oats and molasses to his lucerne hay. 'Don't get used to it but that's a special treat for negotiating all the way up that mountain and back.'

Bonaparte whinnied as if to say thank you.

Millie rubbed their names off the whiteboard and they walked down to the dining room with Susannah. The girls from the sixth grade were gathered around a couple of tables with Miss Reedy holding court.

'Hurry along, Susannah. I want to talk to you all about today's visit to Sainsbury Palace before you have afternoon tea.' She noticed Alice-Miranda and Millie. 'You girls can get something straight away.'

The two younger students gave Miss Reedy a wave and proceeded to the servery, where Mrs Smith was cutting a large marble cake.

'Hello Mrs Smith. That looks delicious.' Alice-Miranda held out her plate and the old woman placed a slab of cake onto it.

'Yes, I hope so. I haven't made too many of these before. It's Mrs Oliver's recipe.'

'Oh, I'm sure it will be lovely.' Alice-Miranda poured two glasses of milk while Millie got her cake too.

'Did you enjoy your ride?' Mrs Smith asked.

'Oh yes, and the sandwiches were perfect, thank you,' Alice-Miranda smiled.

'And how were the sisters?'

'Good,' said Millie.

Mrs Smith raised her nose in the air. 'Oh heavens, I've boiled the pasta dry!' She shot off into the kitchen.

'Let's sit over there.' Millie pointed at the table next to where the sixth-grade girls were talking to Miss Reedy.

'We shouldn't eavesdrop, Millie,' Alice-Miranda admonished.

'Do you really think I was planning to listen to their conversation?' Millie looked shocked.

Alice-Miranda nodded.

'You're right,' Millie said, laughing. 'Come on,

it's not as if the other girls won't tell us later. We'll just hear about it firsthand instead of second.'

Alice-Miranda smiled. 'Only if we can sit on the far end of the table, so you're not completely obvious.' The tiny child followed Millie to the other end of the dining room.

Chapter 20

'I wonder if Ambrosia will give Professor Crookston a piece of her mind when she picks Jacinta up,' Millie asked. 'My mother would be furious if I lost my place before I even started.'

'I can't imagine your mother ever being furious about anything,' Alice-Miranda replied. Pippa McNoughton-McGill was just about the calmest person Alice-Miranda had ever met.

Alice-Miranda and Millie had sat near the older girls during the debriefing with Miss Reedy and Mr Plumpton. All talk of the incident with Professor Crookston and Jacinta had been cut off but there had been a lot of complaining about the mean teachers. It wasn't until the older girls went to get their afternoon tea that Alice-Miranda caught Miss Reedy's eye.

'I'll get us some tea, shall I?' Mr Plumpton asked Miss Reedy before he walked to the servery.

Miss Reedy bit down on her thumbnail. Alice-Miranda had observed that it was something she seemed to do when she was anxious.

'How was your day, Miss Reedy?' Alice-Miranda asked from the adjacent table.

'To be perfectly honest, Alice-Miranda, I've had much better. I suppose you've already heard that there was a bit of trouble with Jacinta,' Miss Reedy replied. She walked over and sat down beside Millie.

Alice-Miranda nodded. 'Susannah came to the stables.'

'Is she expelled?' Millie asked.

'I'm afraid I don't know, Millie. When I said that I'd stay with her until her mother arrived, Mrs Jelly was very firm and told me that wouldn't be necessary. I could hardly bear to leave her there after Mr Plumpton explained what had happened. But

I telephoned Miss Grimm and she said if that's how Mrs Jelly wanted to play things, then so be it.'

'Poor Jacinta,' Alice-Miranda sighed. 'Is she staying with her mother tonight?'

'I'm not sure,' Miss Reedy replied. 'She'll be expected at school first thing tomorrow morning, so it would probably be better if she came back in. I think Mrs Headlington-Bear has a lot on her plate at the moment, since she's helping Mrs Parker too.'

Alice-Miranda looked at the clock on the wall. It was still early enough to walk over to Wisteria Cottage with Millie. 'Could we go and see her at her mother's place?'

Mr Plumpton returned to the table with two teacups and two slices of cake.

'What do you think about the girls going over to Wisteria Cottage to talk to Jacinta, Mr Plumpton?' Miss Reedy asked.

'It couldn't do any harm,' Mr Plumpton agreed.

'We could visit Mrs Parker too and see what she thinks about putting Mr Parker on the cereal boxes,' Millie suggested.

Miss Reedy frowned and sipped her tea. 'What cereal boxes?'

Alice-Miranda explained what she and Millie had been talking about earlier, and their doubts about Mr Parker's disappearance.

'I think that's a wonderful idea,' said Mr Plumpton. 'And I agree with you completely, girls, that we can't be sure what's happened to Mr Parker and the nurse.'

'I just don't want to upset Mrs Parker any more,' Alice-Miranda said. 'I have to telephone Daddy and see if they could do the cereal boxes, but I wanted to ask what she thought first. We'd better go to the house and let Mrs Howard know where we're going,' Alice-Miranda said.

Miss Reedy shook her head. 'Afraid not.'

Millie's brow creased. 'Why?'

'Because one of Mrs Howard's grandchildren had an accident and the poor little girl's been rushed to hospital. Mrs Howard has gone to look after the rest of her grandchildren.'

'Oh, I hope she's going to be all right,' Alice-Miranda said.

'Yes, me too,' Miss Reedy replied. 'I think it was just a broken bone.'

Millie groaned. 'Is Shaker coming to look after us?'

Miss Reedy shook her head. 'I asked if she could come tomorrow but she said that she was going on a cruise.'

'A cruise?' Millie was incredulous. 'But she's, like, a hundred!'

'Millie!' Alice-Miranda giggled. 'Mrs Shakeshaft is nowhere near that old. Besides, there were lots of mature guests at Aunt Charlotte's wedding on the ship and they seemed to enjoy cruising.'

'I suppose so. It's just that I can't really picture her lying about on the pool deck.' Millie giggled and added, 'In a bikini.'

'Heaven forbid,' Mr Plumpton snorted. 'Now that would be sight.'

Miss Reedy elbowed him sharply in the ribs and said, 'Mean! You're both mean. I think it's wonderful that she's going on holiday and doing something for herself – although her timing's a bit rotten. I hope I can be off cruising when I'm a woman of similarly advanced years.'

Mr Plumpton leaned over and whispered in Miss Reedy's ear, 'Yes, but you'd still look lovely in a bikini.' The woman's cheeks looked as if they'd caught alight.

'What did you say, Mr Plumpton?' Millie asked,

glancing at Alice-Miranda. The pair of them smiled at each other.

'Nothing, Millie!' Miss Reedy picked up her teacup and took a small sip. Anyway, I'll be staying at the house until we can find a temporary replacement.'

Alice-Miranda clapped her hands with delight. 'That's wonderful.'

Millie stayed silent. Miss Reedy had been left in charge of the boarding house once before and Millie's memories of that experience were not particularly happy. The woman had made Mrs Howard look like Mary Poppins.

'All right, girls, you go and see Mrs Parker and Jacinta. Just make sure that you're back before half past five,' Miss Reedy instructed.

The two girls stood up, cleared their afternoon tea plates and saucers, and set off for the village.

Chapter 21

Myrtle Parker hadn't been the least bit impressed when Ambrosia Headlington-Bear rushed off shortly after the police left the house on Sunday morning. There was apparently some emergency with that troublesome daughter of hers. Ambrosia was supposed to be helping Myrtle deal with things at home. Not that Myrtle was even sure what all of the 'things' were. The hospital wouldn't send anyone to pick up the bed and the medical equipment for several days. Now Myrtle was at a bit of a loss.

She went to the cupboard to retrieve the telephone book. She flicked it open and soon found the page she was after. *Blackett and Reaper, Funeral Directors.* Reginald might still have been alive somewhere but he was certainly dead to her. A funeral would stop the gossip. Her fingers trembled as she reached out to dial the number.

A deep voice echoed down the line. 'Good afternoon, Blackett and Reaper, funeral directors of distinction, Gilbert Reaper speaking. How may I be of assistance?'

Myrtle gulped. For the first time in a long while she didn't know what to say. She wondered what on earth she was thinking. Reginald wasn't dead. He was alive and she wanted him back.

'May I help you?' the man asked.

Myrtle began to breathe heavily.

'Oh, I say, please don't waste my time. Prank calls are not appreciated.' And with that the man hung up.

Myrtle let out a choked sob and began to wail. 'Reginald!' she cried. 'Reginald, my darling. How could you? I love you so much. I just want you to come home and I promise, no more jobs. Please, just come back to me.'

She stumbled into the front sitting room and clambered onto the empty hospital bed. Myrtle sobbed until finally sleep overtook her.

☆

When Alice-Miranda and Millie arrived at Wisteria Cottage, Ambrosia Headlington-Bear's car was missing from the driveway. The girls headed across the road to Mrs Parker's bungalow.

'The garden's looking good,' said Millie as they walked past the roses in full bloom. 'Pity Mr Parker never got to see it.'

'Maybe he noticed when he left the house,' Alice-Miranda said. She walked up the steps to the porch and rang the bell.

Inside, Myrtle Parker awoke with a start. She wondered for a second where she was, then leapt off the bed as if she'd rolled over and found a python snuggled up beside her. She patted her cheeks and smoothed her dress but didn't bother to look in the mirror. Had she, she might have seen that her helmet-like curls were in rather a mess.

Myrtle thumped across the sitting room and into the hallway, and wrenched open the door. 'What do you want?'

'Hello Mrs Parker. I know you must be feeling terrible but Millie and I wondered if we could talk to you.' Alice-Miranda noticed Myrtle's red-rimmed eyes and the two deep lines that had made their way down her heavily powdered cheeks. 'May we come in please?'

'I suppose so.' Myrtle didn't want to be alone, but she could hardly tell that to two children, could she?

'Would you like me to make you some tea?' Alice-Miranda asked. Then she leaned forward and did something that took Myrtle Parker completely by surprise.

The child wrapped herself around Myrtle's middle and held on tightly.

For a moment the old woman didn't quite know what to do with herself. Then she decided that the best thing would be to hug the girl right back.

'I'm so sorry, Mrs Parker,' Alice-Miranda said.

'Me too,' Millie mumbled from behind her.

'Yes.' Myrtle shuddered and removed herself from Alice-Miranda's grip. 'No point standing out here all day. Come in. I hope you can make a decent pot of tea, young lady.'

Millie smiled up at the woman. 'She's brilliant at it.'

The trio walked down the hallway to the kitchen, where Alice-Miranda told Mrs Parker to take a seat. She put the kettle on and Millie hunted about for some biscuits.

'Mrs Parker, I understand that the police think they know what happened to Mr Parker,' Alice-Miranda said carefully.

Myrtle did her best to maintain a steely expression. She didn't want to fall apart again, especially not in front of children. 'Yes, the police are quite certain they know what's happened to Reginald.'

'Do you really think that Mr Parker would have gone with Nurse Raylene?' Alice-Miranda asked.

'It looks that way. I don't want to talk about this any more, Alice-Miranda. No amount of wishing and hoping is going to bring my Reginald back to me.'

Millie put some shortbread onto a plate. She squeezed Alice-Miranda's arm and whispered, 'It might be best to leave it for now.'

'What are you two whispering about? Don't you know it's the height of rudeness, girls?'

Millie brought some plates and cups and saucers to the table, and Alice-Miranda poured Mrs Parker a strong cup of black tea, and then two weak and milky cups for herself and Millie.

Alice-Miranda decided that she would change her approach. 'Mrs Parker, is there anything we could do to help? Maybe around the house?'

Myrtle suddenly remembered that there was a load of washing in the machine. 'There are some sheets that need to be dried,' she instructed. 'Ambrosia started the job but didn't finish it. She had to race off – something about that rotten child of hers getting into trouble.'

'Jacinta's not rotten,' Millie said.

Mrs Parker pursed her lips. 'Yes, well, I'll be the judge of that.'

'I can deal with the sheets,' Alice-Miranda volunteered. She walked into the utility room off the side of the kitchen. 'Shall I put them on the line?'

'I'll help.' Millie began to slide down from her seat.

'No, Millicent, you stay right there. I'd like some company,' Myrtle ordered. Then she raised her voice. 'Alice-Miranda, just pop the sheets into the dryer. You won't be able to reach the clothes line and the last thing I need is you falling off a chair in the back garden.'

Millie curled her lip and sat back down.

Alice-Miranda poked her head out of the utility

room. 'I'm afraid that the sheets didn't quite make it into the washing machine,' she said.

'Urgh. It's so hard to get good help,' Myrtle tutted under her breath. 'Do you know how to do it?'

'Yes, Mrs Parker. Mrs Shillingsworth taught me how to use the machine at home,' Alice-Miranda called back.

The child picked up the sheets and began to pile them into the front loader. Something fell onto the floor at her feet. It was an envelope addressed to Mrs Parker but there was no stamp or address.

Alice-Miranda finished putting the washing on, and walked back into the kitchen. 'Mrs Parker, I found this.' She handed Myrtle the envelope.

The old woman frowned and turned it over. 'Where did it come from?'

'It was just among the sheets.'

Millie sipped her tea and watched as Myrtle Parker tore at the envelope. She unfolded a small letter.

'Get me my glasses, Alice-Miranda,' she ordered. 'They're on my bedside table.'

Alice-Miranda returned from the bedroom empty-handed.

'I'm afraid I couldn't find them,' she said.

'Well, have a look around here,' Myrtle bossed. 'They can't have gone too far.'

Alice-Miranda walked around the kitchen, into the sitting room and the dining room, but couldn't see Mrs Parker's glasses anywhere.

'Well, I can't read the jolly thing without them. Here,' Myrtle sniffed, and handed the letter to Millie. 'Read it to me.'

Millie began:

Dear Mrs Parker,

I have had the worst news from home this morning and have to go immediately to see my father, who is very unwell. The doctors have warned that he might not make it to the end of the week. I am very sorry to leave Mr Parker unattended but you said that you would only be a short while and it's now been a long while. And as we're on the subject, you do that quite a lot. I have borrowed Mr Parker's watch because mine has stopped and I will return it when I am able to come back to work. Then perhaps you should use it because it seems your watch isn't especially reliable.

I am meeting my brother and we will head north together.

Mr Parker was looking particularly good this morning. He smiled several times and at one stage I thought he opened his eyes. He is getting much stronger every day and I think he could be up and about before you know it. Wouldn't that be a blessing?

Yours sincerely,
Raylene Cross
Nursing Sister

PS I have taken that bag of Mr Parker's clothes that you asked me to give to the charity shop. I'll drop them off when I get a chance.

Alice-Miranda's eyes were like dinner plates. 'Mrs Parker, did you hear that? Mr Parker didn't go with Nurse Raylene at all.'

'Wow!' Millie exclaimed. 'That's incredible. Mr Parker's out there somewhere.'

'Mrs Parker, you should call Constable Derby right away.' Alice-Miranda clapped her hands together.

But that wasn't going to happen. There was a loud thump as Myrtle Parker's head glanced off the plate and onto the kitchen table. The shock had knocked her out cold.

Chapter 22

Alice-Miranda raced to Myrtle's side. She checked that she was still breathing and then said, 'I think she's fainted. Millie, can you call Constable Derby and let him know what we've found – and tell him that Mrs Parker has fainted too?'

Millie went to the telephone and dialled for the police. Mrs Parker had one of those ancient handsets that was still attached to the wall. The phone rang for ages before finally someone picked it up.

'Hello Mrs Derby, it's Millie. Is Constable Derby there? I need to talk to him about Mr Parker. And Mrs Parker has fainted,' Millie babbled.

There was a pause as she listened to Mrs Derby on the other end of the line.

'So, when will he be back?' the child asked. 'Please tell him to come as soon as he can. It's very good news. Mr Parker didn't go with Nurse Raylene at all. Alice-Miranda found a note.'

Alice-Miranda could hear Mrs Derby's excited voice through the telephone.

'That's a good idea. I'll call Miss Grimm straight away.' Millie hung up the phone.

Alice-Miranda looked up from where she was patting Mrs Parker gently on the cheek. 'What did she say?'

'Constable Derby is at the railway station talking to the detectives there but Mrs Derby's going to call and let him know what we found. He could be a while so we should see if someone from school can come over and help with Mrs Parker.'

Alice-Miranda nodded. 'Why don't you go and see if Mrs Headlington-Bear is home yet? I'll stay here.'

Millie agreed and immediately set off across the road.

Ambrosia's shiny sports car was just turning into the driveway. Jacinta was sitting in the passenger seat with a face like thunder.

The driver's door opened and Millie flew around to greet Ambrosia.

'Hello Millie,' the woman said, then whispered, 'I don't think Jacinta's in the mood to play.'

Jacinta got out of the car and slammed the door, then stalked into the house without giving Millie a second glance.

'It's not that,' Millie blurted. 'It's Mrs Parker.'

'What's happened now?' Ambrosia's day had gone from bad to worse. She had been looking forward to a cup of tea and a lie-down before getting on with the article she was writing for Highton's. She hadn't missed a deadline yet and she wasn't about to start.

'She's fainted,' Millie said.

'Oh!' Ambrosia clutched a hand to her chest. She took off across the road towards Myrtle's bungalow, with Millie scrambling beside her.

'And she was really mad that you hadn't put the sheets into the wash –' Millie began.

Ambrosia huffed and cut her off. 'Was she? I don't know how I've come to be her personal slave.'

'No, you don't understand, it was the best thing that could have happened! When Alice-Miranda went to do the washing, she shook the sheets and a letter fell out,' Millie continued.

'What letter?'

'A letter from Nurse Raylene saying that she'd gone home to see her father,' Millie explained.

'But why did she take Mr Parker with her?' Ambrosia asked.

'She didn't. He was still here when she left, and she said that she thought he was getting much better.'

Ambrosia's eyes widened. 'So Mr Parker didn't run off with the nurse?'

'No. He's just missing.'

Ambrosia opened Myrtle's front door and raced to the kitchen, where Mrs Parker was making groaning noises.

She rushed to the woman's side. 'Oh Myrtle, this is wonderful news!'

Myrtle lifted her head off the table and rubbed the side of her forehead. 'What are you talking about?' she growled.

A sharp memory pierced the fog that shrouded Myrtle's head. Had she dreamt it or had the child just read something about Reginald?

'Reginald?' For a moment Myrtle Parker sat absolutely still, as she tried to remember what had sent her into a spin. 'Well, don't just stand there,' she ordered as the letter's contents came flooding back to her. 'Call Constable Derby. Tell the man to get the search teams together. Put out that ABC again. My Reginald is close by and we need to find him.'

Alice-Miranda smiled. 'That's the spirit, Mrs Parker.'

'Constable Derby won't be back until later this evening,' Millie said. 'I've already talked with Mrs Derby.'

'And what did the woman suggest we do?' Myrtle demanded.

'Find someone to help us look after you,' Millie replied.

'What? I don't need looking after. I'm not an invalid, you know!' Myrtle crowed.

And with that, she stood up and smoothed the front of her floral dress, marched to the sideboard and picked up her hat. She jammed it onto her head and scooped up her handbag.

'Myrtle, what are you doing?' said Ambrosia.

'What does it look like?' Myrtle sniffed. 'I'm going out.'

'Yes, I can see that, but where are you going?'

'I'm going to find my husband.' Myrtle turned on her low brown heels and stormed down the hallway. 'And I'd appreciate some help if any of you could be bothered to come along.'

Alice-Miranda, Millie and Ambrosia all looked at one another.

'I think she's lost it,' Millie whispered.

Ambrosia thought the same thing.

'Perhaps you should go with her, Mrs Headlington-Bear. Millie and I will go and see if we can get Jacinta to come back to school with us,' Alice-Miranda suggested. She wanted to look for Mr Parker but she was worried about Jacinta too.

'Yes. It's not as if the police haven't looked for Mr Parker already. He really could be anywhere by now,' Ambrosia agreed.

'You should call your father and get him to put Mr Parker on the cereal boxes,' Millie said.

Ambrosia looked at the girls in confusion and then shook her head. 'Never mind. Let's go.'

For all her striding and harrumphing, Myrtle Parker had only got as far as the front door. 'Well,' she called, 'is anyone coming with me or do I have to go on my own – again?'

Ambrosia Headlington-Bear sighed then called out, 'I'm coming, Myrtle.'

Alice-Miranda and Millie followed the women down the driveway. Myrtle Parker hopped into her car and turned the key in the ignition while Ambrosia was still closing the passenger door. Alice-Miranda tapped on the driver's window and Mrs Parker wound it down.

'Mrs Parker, did Mr Parker have any special friends in the village before he got sick?' she asked.

Myrtle shook her head. 'Reginald didn't have any friends except me. He was a very private man. Anyway, he had far too many things to do around here to be out socialising.'

But that wasn't entirely true.

'Oh,' Alice-Miranda said with a frown. She was sorry to hear that. She'd often imagined Mr Parker being quite outgoing and funny.

'Good luck,' Millie said as Myrtle began to back down the driveway.

The two girls waved and watched as the car puttered along the lane.

'I hope they find him,' Millie said.

'Me too,' Alice-Miranda agreed. But she had

a strange feeling that they wouldn't be seeing Mr Parker for a little while yet.

'Come on, let's go and see the pyromaniac,' Millie said.

Alice-Miranda looked at her friend reproachfully. 'Millie, please don't say anything to upset her.'

'She's already upset. Nothing I say will make a difference,' Millie said.

'Don't be so sure of that,' Alice-Miranda replied.

'If you say so. But you can go in first. If she's going to rip someone's head off, it's not going to be mine.'

Chapter 23

At home, Silas Wiley changed into his new purple jogging suit. He retrieved the little jar from his jacket pocket and took it downstairs to the kitchen, where he hid it in the cupboard among the jams and peanut butter.

'Safe as houses,' he muttered.

He took a water bottle from the fridge, snatched his keys from the bench and jogged down the hallway to the front door. For the past few months he'd gone running every day and was surprised by how much better it was making him feel – even if he had struggled to run more than a hundred metres at first.

The front gate banged as he took off down the street towards the huge park on the edge of Downsfordvale. The afternoon sun beat down on his back and tiny beads of perspiration formed on his brow. As he ran, Silas wondered how he should deliver the good news about his discovery to Finley Spencer. Although he hadn't actually spoken with the owner, surely Finley would be more than happy about what he'd learned and they could sort out the details with the old fellow soon enough. He thought about telephoning her when he got home but decided that was the least dramatic option.

Perhaps he should play it cool and ask for a meeting. Maybe she'd send the helicopter to pick him up. Wouldn't that make the plebs at the council green with envy? Silas had never ridden in a chopper but he'd always considered it the domain of the super-successful. And Finley Spencer was certainly that.

He turned into the park and started down the perimeter track, completely lost in his own thoughts. Silas ran past a blur of pastel-clad joggers but when he tripped on a stone he was jolted back to the present. A woman was running towards him.

'Ursula.' Silas crossed to the other side of the path and almost bumped into her.

Ursula pulled her earphones out. 'Oh, Mayor Wiley, I didn't realise you ran in the afternoons now as well,' she puffed.

Silas was trying hard to calm his breathing too. 'Yes, yes, Urs. Morning, evening, noon, night. I just love it and we all know the results, don't we?' He smiled at her and patted his almost flat stomach.

Ursula had to stop herself laughing out loud. She'd never met such a vain man in all her life. 'I'll leave you to get on with it then,' she spluttered and turned to head off in the opposite direction.

'No, wait, Urs. Um, I was just about to head back that way myself.' Silas turned around while jogging up and down on the spot.

'But I thought you always ran in the same direction around the park.' Ursula had often heard her boss boasting of his athletic prowess and the exact route he took through the park. Boring as his nattering was, she was grateful for it, as it had allowed her to completely avoid the situation she now found herself in. Ursula turned a grimace into a smile. 'Of course, sir.'

'Urs, you really must stop all this "sir" and

"Mayor Wiley" business when we're out of the office. Call me Silas, for heaven's sake. Anyway, Urs, I wanted to talk to you about something, so it's wonderful that we've bumped into each other,' Silas gabbled as they began running again.

'Oh?'

He flashed a grin. 'It's to do with Finley Spencer.'

Ursula frowned. She wondered why his news couldn't wait until they were in the office tomorrow.

'You mustn't share this with anyone,' Silas instructed.

She nodded. If there was one thing Ursula was very good at, it was keeping secrets.

'Finley Spencer wanted me to help her get some old fogey over at Winchesterfield to sell her his land. She's keen on a new housing development – you know she's such a forward thinker. I suspect there will be plans for a giant shopping complex and the like,' Silas prattled. 'It will be good for the district.'

Ursula nodded, although she didn't think there were many developments that were particularly good for the district.

'Well, I went over to see the fellow this morning.'

'And was he agreeable?' she asked.

'Heavens, no. I didn't even meet him. There was no one about. But I discovered something that could really set the cat among the pigeons, Urs. Just wait until you hear this . . .'

Ursula listened to her boss's tale and wondered exactly what he planned to do with all of this information.

'So you can imagine just how grateful Finley Spencer will be,' Silas said. 'But I'd like to do a little bit more research and then I have to decide on the perfect way to tell her. I want her to know just how much trouble I've gone to for this deal.'

Ursula lengthened her stride. As she was quite a bit taller than Silas, he struggled to keep up. 'But you don't even know if the man is willing to sell the land.'

'I'm sure Finley will pay him handsomely for it, especially once she knows what's out there,' Silas replied.

But Ursula wasn't so sure. Spencer Industries was a giant company and had a reputation for steamrolling its opposition. The poor man probably didn't have a hope. And as for going to a lot of trouble, it sounded like Silas had stumbled on the information quite by chance.

'Anyway, Urs, I wanted your advice. Do you

think I should telephone Finley and tell her the good news or should I invite her in? Or perhaps I should suggest we meet in private – and then maybe she'll send the helicopter for me.'

Ursula shrugged. How would she know what he should do? 'Whereabouts is the land?'

Silas attempted a suave raise of his eyebrows. 'If I told you, Urs, I might have to kill you.'

Ursula rolled her eyes. 'Really? I don't think that would do your re-election prospects any good.'

'Well, so long as we're running under the council cone of silence, the land is deep in the woods on the other side of Winchesterfield.'

Ursula coughed and seemed unable to catch her breath.

Silas wondered if she'd finally run out of puff. 'Would you like to take a break?'

'I'm fine. Does this place in the woods have a name?' she gasped.

'Wood End. It's owned by some old-timer. According to the information from Finley, the wife died a few years ago and he won't be far behind her.'

Ursula began to cough again. Her heart was hammering inside her chest and beads of perspiration trickled down her face. She stopped suddenly, leaving Silas a few steps ahead.

He turned and looked at her. 'Is something wrong?'

Ursula doubled over. 'Just something in my throat.'

'Come and sit down.' Silas guided her to a nearby park bench, where she buried her head in her hands. 'What can I do?' Silas wasn't used to looking after anyone.

'I'm fine,' Ursula managed to get out between coughs. She gathered herself together and stood up. 'I think I might head home, if that's all right, sir.'

'Silas,' he tutted. 'Are you sure you can manage on your own?'

Ursula nodded and Silas felt a pang of relief. He didn't want to catch anything.

'If you're not well in the morning, don't come into the office. And please see the doctor. You know I can't afford to get sick. My schedule doesn't allow for days off, Urs.'

Ursula had to look away. She felt like giving him a clout over his senseless head.

'I'll see you in the morning.' She set off across the park, not looking back.

Silas set off again too, but at a much slower pace. Ursula hadn't been any help at all, so he still hadn't decided what he'd do about telling Finley Spencer. She would be grateful, very grateful, he was sure. She said herself that people in her industry were richly rewarded. And he was positive that the information he had would make her very pleased indeed.

Chapter 24

Millie and Alice-Miranda knocked on the back door of Wisteria Cottage before letting themselves inside.

'Hello Jacinta?' Alice-Miranda called.

The house was silent apart from the noise of a television in another room.

The girls made their way through the gleaming white kitchen and down the hallway to the front sitting room. Jacinta was lying on the white leather couch stuffing her face with crisps while *Winners Are Grinners* blared from the television.

'Hello.' Alice-Miranda walked around and stood in front of her.

Jacinta didn't reply. She craned her neck to see past her visitor.

'We heard about what happened today. Are you all right?' Alice-Miranda asked. But she already knew the answer to that question.

'Would you mind moving? I'm watching that,' Jacinta snapped and shovelled another handful of crisps into her mouth.

Something was terribly wrong, thought Alice-Miranda. Jacinta didn't eat junk food. Of all the girls at school, she was by far the most health conscious.

Millie was observing Alice-Miranda's attempts to talk to Jacinta from behind the couch.

Alice-Miranda decided on a different approach. 'We've come to walk back to school with you.'

Jacinta shook her head.

'Miss Reedy said that you should come back with us,' Alice-Miranda explained.

'I'm not going,' said Jacinta tersely.

'But you have to be back for lessons in the morning, and your mother and Mrs Parker have gone out to look for Mr Parker again, so you shouldn't stay here on your own,' said Alice-Miranda patiently.

Jacinta looked up, puzzled. 'But Mr Parker's run away with his nurse.'

'No, he didn't. We found a note from Nurse Raylene. It looks as if he's woken up and wandered off somewhere.'

'Well, you'd better go and help with the search,' Jacinta said, deadpan.

Millie was growing more and more tired of Jacinta's behaviour. She stalked around to the front of the couch and further blocked the girl's view.

'Come on, Jacinta, let's go,' Millie said. 'You're being ridiculous. We heard how mean that teacher was to you, and giving him a piece of your mind was completely understandable. I think it was brave actually, standing up for yourself and the other girls. But now you're being stupid.'

Jacinta sat up and put the bowl down beside her. 'Am not!' she spat.

Millie rounded on the older girl. 'Yes, you are. Alice-Miranda is trying to be kind but you're being rude to her. She doesn't deserve it. Frankly, I don't care if you want to be foul – we were all used to it before. But what I don't understand is how you could have pretended to be nice for so long now when really you're just the same spoiled brat you always were.'

'You don't know anything, Millie.' Jacinta stormed off to her bedroom and slammed the door.

Millie looked at Alice-Miranda and shrugged. 'Let's go. Obviously she doesn't want to come back with us.'

Alice-Miranda frowned. This wasn't like Jacinta at all. If this is what growing up did to you, she rather hoped to stay a little girl forever.

'I'm going to try one last time,' she said, and raced off down the hallway.

She knocked at the door and poked her head inside. Jacinta was lying on her bed. Alice-Miranda sat down beside her and reached out to stroke the girl's shoulder.

'Go away!'

'But you're upset and I want to help,' Alice-Miranda replied.

'Well, this time you can't.'

Alice-Miranda paused for a moment before taking a deep breath. 'I can't if you won't tell me what's wrong.'

'I don't want to tell you. It's none of your business, even though you think you can go around saving the world and making everything better.

You can't, you know. There are some things that you can't change, even with all your money.'

'It's not *my* money, Jacinta, it's my parents'.'

'You won't understand anyway,' Jacinta said. 'You've never done anything bad in your life. You're perfect and everyone knows it.'

Alice-Miranda shook her head. 'No, I'm not. And I'm sure that Miss Grimm will understand that the fire was an accident.'

'Just go back to school and leave me alone,' Jacinta fumed. 'Everything's ruined.'

Alice-Miranda stood up. It was clear that Jacinta was not ready to talk about whatever was troubling her. 'Well, you know where to find me.'

Jacinta heard the door close. A silent tear slid down her cheek. She couldn't believe what she'd just done. Alice-Miranda was the best friend she'd ever had. Her plan wasn't meant to go like this at all. She hadn't meant for the other girls to be involved. This was about her and her alone. But she'd set the wheels in motion and she was going to see it through no matter what.

Alice-Miranda found Millie watching television in the front room.

Millie looked up. 'I gather that didn't go well.' Alice-Miranda shook her head.

Millie glanced at the clock on the wall. It was already after five. 'Come on, we'd better get back.'

The girls walked along the hall.

'Bye Jacinta,' Alice-Miranda called. But Jacinta didn't hear a thing. Her head was stuffed under her pillow and she was silently sobbing her heart out.

Chapter 25

Alice-Miranda and Millie arrived back at Grimthorpe House just before half past five. Miss Reedy was already storming through the building barking orders at girls to clean up their rooms and make sure their uniforms were ready for the morning.

Millie had warned Alice-Miranda on the return trip that having Miss Reedy in the boarding house was not going to be much fun.

The woman intercepted the pair as they came in the back door. 'Oh, hello there, girls. Where's Jacinta?'

'I'm sorry, Miss Reedy, but she didn't want to come back with us,' said Alice-Miranda.

Livinia Reedy frowned and a deep line formed from the tip of eyebrow to the top of her nose. 'Well, she'd better be here first thing in the morning, as Miss Grimm would like a word.'

'I'm sure she will. We have some good news too,' Alice-Miranda fizzed. 'Mr Parker didn't run away. I found a note in the washing at Mrs Parker's house. Nurse Raylene has gone to visit her father and when she left Mr Parker was still there.'

'Oh, that's wonderful. What a relief,' Miss Reedy said. 'I imagine the search parties will be back out looking for him then.'

'Yes,' Alice-Miranda nodded. 'Can we tell the girls and go out after dinner to help for a little while?'

Miss Reedy thought about it for a moment, and then shook her head. 'I think we should leave it to the police. There's not enough time to send the girls out far and if he was on school property, surely Charlie would have spotted him by now.'

'But there are the woods and the mountain too,' Millie protested. 'He might have wandered up there.'

'Are you sure we can't go out, Miss Reedy?'

Alice-Miranda persisted. She had a feeling that Mr Parker wasn't far away at all.

'No girls, not tonight. You need to make sure you've got everything ready for the morning. I won't have any fussing.' Miss Reedy spotted Sloane about to dump an armload of washing onto the couch in front of the television. 'Sloane Sykes, you take that to your room and fold it!'

'But Miss Reedy, we always fold our washing in front of the TV,' Sloane griped.

'Not on my watch, young lady. Off you go.' Miss Reedy strode towards the girl and ushered her down the hall.

'I told you she was bossy,' Millie said.

'Come on, let's go to our room,' Alice-Miranda replied. 'I'm sure we can go out riding tomorrow after school and help look for Mr Parker.'

Millie shook her head. 'We've got a singing rehearsal for the end-of-year celebration.'

'Oh, of course.' Alice-Miranda frowned, wondering when they'd next have an opportunity to help with the search.

'Oh no,' Millie groaned suddenly.

'What's the matter?' Alice-Miranda asked.

'I forgot to do my English homework for Miss

Reedy. She knows we've been out for most of the weekend and now she'll kill me if I don't have it finished.'

'Come on then, I'll help you if I can,' Alice-Miranda offered.

Millie felt better already – if anyone knew the difference between nouns, verbs, adjectives and adverbs, it was Alice-Miranda.

★

Monday morning came and went in a blur. Miss Reedy had the girls up and out of the house even earlier than Mrs Howard usually did. Sloane received a solid telling off for forgetting her English books and having to go back to the house after breakfast. Miss Reedy felt compelled to go with her, lest she get any ideas about staying in on her own for the day.

There was no sign of Jacinta.

At the morning assembly, Miss Grimm announced that the police were still looking for Mr Parker. A murmur went through the hall, as the girls whispered about getting a day off class to join the search. But Miss Grimm said that the police were handling the matter and she and Professor Winterbottom had decided it would be best to send a group of cadets from Fayle out to look in some of the more remote areas. There was a collective groan from the girls.

Millie nudged Alice-Miranda as she spotted Jacinta skulking into the back of the assembly hall.

Miss Grimm had seen her too. 'Girls, I would like to remind you all, and particularly the students in the sixth grade, that although there are only a few weeks of school left for the year, I expect everyone to continue to uphold the high standards of Winchesterfield-Downsfordvale. Just because you are leaving soon, you do not have licence to behave badly. If you believe otherwise, I suspect we might keep you here for another year.'

Miss Grimm's final comment was met with a cheer from the girls of the sixth grade. She hadn't been expecting quite that reaction and smiled in reply.

'We'd love to stay. Professor Crookston is the meanest teacher I've ever met,' Madeline Bloom called out.

Miss Grimm looked as if she'd swallowed a fly. Madeline was one of the quietest students in the year.

'Life is full of surprises, girls.' She arched an

eyebrow. 'And to that end I would like to see Jacinta Headlington-Bear in my office immediately after this assembly.'

Sloane leaned over and whispered to Alice-Miranda and Millie, 'She's going to cop it.'

'Do you have something to add, Miss Sykes?' Miss Grimm's apparently bionic hearing had kicked in again.

Sloane blushed as if she'd been caught with her hand in the biscuit barrel. 'No, Miss Grimm. But from what I've heard, it wasn't Jacinta's fault. That teacher was horrid and he pushed her into it.'

Ophelia Grimm glared at the girl. She couldn't have been more thrilled to see the creeping red flush lighting up Sloane's cheeks. It seemed that Sloane was beginning to understand the difference between right and wrong. Ophelia didn't say another word, but merely gestured for Miss Reedy to conclude the assembly with the day's announcements.

The English teacher moved to the podium as the headmistress returned to her seat. 'Girls, please ensure that you are all on time to the rehearsal this afternoon. Mr Trout and I are looking forward to the Summer Spectacular living up to its name.' Privately, Miss Reedy feared it would amount to a summer spectacle rather than a spectacular, as they'd had nowhere near enough time to rehearse the skits and the songs.

Mrs Derby appeared at the side of the stage, looking anxious. She seemed to be trying to get Miss Grimm's attention.

'Please stand while we sing the school song,' Miss Reedy instructed. The whole hall rose in one movement' and Mr Trout began his extravagant introduction on the organ.

Ophelia Grimm flinched. She wished he could manage an abridged version and stop that infernal showing off.

Millie prodded Alice-Miranda and the two girls giggled. Miss Grimm's face said it all.

Whatever news Mrs Derby had to deliver clearly couldn't wait; she scurried across the stage and pushed a piece of paper between Miss Grimm and Danika, the Head Prefect.

'Something's going on,' Millie whispered.

Miss Grimm glanced down at the note then turned to Mrs Derby. 'They can't be serious!' she roared. Realising there were one hundred eyes trained on her, she turned back to the children, gulped and began singing at the top of her lungs.

Mrs Derby raised her eyebrows and retreated to the side of the stage.

As the teachers filed out of the hall with Miss Grimm in the lead, Alice-Miranda noticed that the headmistress seemed to be striding at twice her usual pace. After she passed the children, her smile evaporated and even over the din of the singing and organ accompaniment, the tripping of her high heels as she ran across the courtyard was audible.

'Something's happened,' Millie said to Alice-Miranda. 'She looked like she was about to explode.'

Alice-Miranda nodded. 'I wonder what.'

'Jacinta's probably been expelled from Sainsbury Palace,' Sloane announced.

Alice-Miranda turned to look at her. 'I hope not.'

'Who knows?' Millie shrugged. 'But I think I'll stay out of Miss Grimm's way today.'

Chapter 26

Silas Wiley turned the card over in his hand. He reached for the telephone and dialled the number, not expecting Finley Spencer to answer the call herself.

'Hello Silas, lovely to hear from you,' she cooed.

Silas's chest puffed out and a sickly grin spread across his face. 'Good morning, Finley, it's *lovely* to talk to you again.'

'I gather you have some good news for me.'

'Yes, but I thought you might want to speak face to face, rather than on the telephone. You never know who might be listening,' Silas said cautiously.

'I'm afraid I have a rather full schedule, Silas. Did you make contact with the owner of the property?' The honey had disappeared from Finley's tone – her fascination with him seemed to be evaporating with every passing second.

Silas cleared his throat. 'Actually, no, I didn't.'

The line went silent for an uncomfortably long period.

'I see. Then I gather you're not interested in assisting me.' Finley's voice cut the air like a razor blade.

'Oh, not at all. Of course I want to help you. I didn't see the owner but I did make a rather remarkable discovery.' Silas fidgeted with the phone cord. He wanted this to be as tantalising as possible.

'Yes?'

'I think you'll be more than pleased,' Silas added.

'Well, what is it? What did you find?'

'Um, well, I think we'd better meet in person. I . . . I don't feel I can say it now.'

'Unless you've discovered a goldmine, I think right now is the perfect time to tell me,' Finley Spencer barked.

Silas giggled nervously.

'Are you still there, Silas?' Finley sighed. She'd

known he was a buffoon from the minute she'd laid eyes on him.

Silas gulped. 'I think we need to meet.'

'Fine then,' she huffed. 'I'm sure if you have such incredible news you won't mind taking a little drive.'

'Of course.' Silas's face fell. He'd been waiting for her to offer to send the helicopter.

'My office, in an hour.' She slammed the phone down.

Silas wondered where that was. He turned over the card. There was no address.

He pressed the intercom system. 'Ursula, could you come in here please?' he snapped.

But there was no response. 'Urs, I need some help in here. Now!'

Silas waited another few seconds then stood up and walked to the door. He wrenched it open. Her chair was empty. Of course. Ursula hadn't come in because he'd told her not to if she was sick and she'd called to say that she wasn't well.

Silas went back to the computer and searched for Spencer Industries. The headquarters were in Parsley Vale, and by Silas's calculations it would take him a lot longer than an hour to get there.

'Stupid woman,' he blustered. 'I don't see why

she couldn't come to me. Or send me a faster way of getting there.' He remembered that he had no petrol in the car either and would have to fill up on the way. That would add another ten minutes to the trip.

Silas grabbed his jacket and put it on. He ran through the building with his head down, eager not to be cornered by anyone. He got to the car and, after shoving his hands in every pocket, realised that he'd left his keys sitting on his desk – and he'd slammed the office door, which would of course be locked.

'Argh!' He kicked the car tyres and pounded his fists on the window before rushing back across the car park and down the hall to his office.

Today wasn't going at all as he'd imagined.

☆

Ursula felt as if her stomach could turn inside out at any moment. No doubt Silas wouldn't be pleased by her absence, as he could barely do anything for himself. It had taken him a month to master the intercom under her tutelage. It was no wonder he'd been through two assistants before her – and he'd been the mayor for less than a year.

She sat in her flat going over and over the

information in her head. Could any of it be true?

Silas was convinced that Finley Spencer was a reasonable woman, but Ursula didn't share his confidence. She seemed as if she could manipulate a man to do anything. And Silas was so easily impressed.

Ursula pulled out a piece of paper from her desk drawer and began to write. She paused, wondering how much detail to go into, and decided to keep it short and straight to the point. Very businesslike. Half an hour later, she folded the letter and stuffed it into an envelope.

She made a snap decision, snatching up her car keys and handbag and heading for the door. Then she remembered something that might come in handy and ran back to her bedroom. She opened the wardrobe, pulled out a small case, and slung it over her shoulder. She made her way out through the front gate, hopped into the little red sedan and pulled onto the road.

As she turned onto the high street, Ursula ducked her head. Silas Wiley was filling up his black hatchback at the service station. She hoped that he hadn't seen her. Then she wondered where he was going. He didn't have any appointments out of the office that day.

Ursula planted her foot on the accelerator and sped towards the edge of town.

*

Silas Wiley couldn't believe that his luck could get any worse that day. But it did. He cursed the elderly couple towing the caravan in front of him, and when he finally managed to get past, he caught up to a lorry packed to the gunwales with cattle who seemed to have a collective case of the trots. He hit the windscreen wiper lever and immediately regretted that decision, as there was no water left in the wiper tank. Now he could barely see and the stench of the manure was seeping through the air-conditioning vents, causing him to retch. Silas dropped back to avoid another deposit hitting the windscreen and swore to himself.

When he finally reached Parsley Vale, the GPS guided him to a residential street. He drove up and down before locating number 66. He managed to find a parking spot quite a distance up the road and couldn't believe it when the door was answered by a woman of advanced years, who obviously needed new batteries in her hearing aid.

After quite a bit of yelling, he worked out that he'd punched the wrong address into the contraption. Instead of 66 Red Robin Crescent, he should have been at 66 Red Robin Lane. Silas wondered what sort of idiotic council would approve two roads with the same name in the one town. He certainly wouldn't. When he finally pulled up outside a very modern-looking building in the middle of town, he couldn't help thinking how out of place it looked among the period townhouses that lined the street. A small polished metal plaque on the side of the door declared that he had found Spencer Industries.

He looked at his watch. It was almost two hours since he'd spoken with Finley Spencer. Surely she'd be so grateful for what he had to tell her that she'd forget about his being late.

Silas parked the car in the first available spot and walked the short distance to the office. He smoothed his hair and fixed his collar and, after sniffing his armpits, wished he'd had some deodorant in the glove box. He hoped she wouldn't notice.

Inside, he was confronted by a stark white room furnished with a couple of low white leather chairs. There was no sign of any reception area. He stood for a moment, waiting to see if anyone would appear, then he called out, 'Hello, is anyone here?'

Silas almost leapt through the roof when the opaque glass wall in front of him turned clear, revealing a reception desk with a young woman behind it. The glass wall then lowered to half-height.

'Hello,' the woman said coolly. 'You must be Mr Wiley.'

Silas tried to regain his composure. 'Uh, yes. I didn't see you there.'

'Yes,' she said. 'That's just the point.'

'I see.'

'Yes, you do now.'

The girl seemed to be playing with him and he wasn't the least bit impressed. He glared at her and snapped, 'I have an appointment with Ms Spencer.'

'Yes, we were was expecting you an hour ago,' the woman replied.

'I would have been here an hour ago if it weren't physically impossible to get here in that time – unless of course you have a helicopter at your disposal.'

The young woman smiled. 'I'm afraid that Ms Spencer has been called away on other business.'

'What do you mean "called away"?' Silas could feel his temperature rising. 'I have something very important to discuss with her.'

'I'm terribly sorry, but Ms Spencer is a busy woman and she can't sit around waiting all day,' the receptionist replied sternly. He clearly wasn't the first person she'd dealt with in this way. She held up a small envelope. 'She asked me to give you this.'

Silas tore it open and unfolded the note.

Dear Mr Wiley,

Thank you for your attempts to contact the owners of Wood End. This morning I have decided not to pursue that opportunity as a much larger and more profitable venture has become available to me. I trust that you enjoyed the drive to Parsley Vale. At least it would have been a nice change from being stuck in the office. Whatever it was that you had to tell me in person, I'm sure that you can use to your own advantage. I do admire a man interested in bettering himself. Perhaps one day we can do business together.

Enjoy your return trip.

Yours sincerely,
Finley Spencer

Silas felt as if his head might explode. There was nothing sincere about that woman. How dare she do this to him?

'Is everything all right, Mr Wiley?' the receptionist asked sweetly.

'No, everything is not all right. I have just driven two hours to get here and Ms Spencer has the audacity to give me this,' he huffed.

'But I'm sure that you of all people can appreciate that when an opportunity arises you have to grab it with both hands.'

'Yes, well, I had an amazing opportunity for Ms Spencer but she's chosen to ignore it,' Silas blustered. 'I might just have to take it up on my own.' He stopped suddenly and stood there, blinking.

'Are you all right, Mr Wiley?'

Silas nodded. 'Yes . . . yes, I think I am.' He turned to leave then stopped. 'Tell Ms Spencer that I said thank you for her note and perhaps one day we will be in a position to work together again.'

The receptionist frowned. 'Certainly, sir.' She wondered what had just happened. One minute the man looked ready to kill someone and now he looked like the cat who got the cream.

Silas walked to the door and glanced back as he

pulled it open. 'Can you tell me if there's a mining registry office in Parsley Vale?'

'Yes, Mr Wiley, just around the corner in the high street,' the woman replied.

Silas grinned. 'Wonderful.'

Perhaps it was his lucky day after all.

Chapter 27

Alice-Miranda and Millie had met in the dining room for lunch. Sloane appeared a few minutes later but Jacinta was still nowhere to be seen.

Alice-Miranda decided to check with Jacinta's classmates. 'Excuse me, Susannah,' she said as she approached the older girl. 'Have you seen Jacinta?'

Susannah shook her head. 'She hasn't been in class at all this morning. I saw her heading towards the office straight after the assembly but she hasn't come back.'

Alice-Miranda was worried. After Jacinta's awful time at Sainsbury Palace and her reaction when the girls had visited her at Wisteria Cottage, she wasn't in a good way at all. If she'd been grilled by Miss Grimm for hours, Alice-Miranda could only imagine the state she'd be in now.

'Come on, Millie, let's go and find her.' The tiny child tugged on Millie's tunic sleeve.

'But I'm starving,' Millie said. 'And it's cheesy lasagne day.'

'I'll come,' Sloane offered.

'Oh, all right,' said Millie. 'I'll come too. As long as you promise we'll be back before the end of lunch. I don't want to miss out.'

Alice-Miranda nodded.

The three girls made their way out of the dining room and across the cobblestoned courtyard. Miss Grimm's study was in the oldest part of the school, Winchesterfield Manor. They arrived at the school secretary's office, only to find it empty. There was no sign of Jacinta either.

'What are you doing?' Sloane asked as Alice-Miranda approached the double doors that led to Miss Grimm's study.

'Going to see Miss Grimm,' she answered.

'But she might be busy,' Sloane said. Although Miss Grimm was now perfectly lovely and approachable, she was still the headmistress and Sloane had some nerve-racking memories of being on the other side of that door.

From inside the study there was a loud thump and the girls all jumped. Miss Grimm's voice penetrated the thick walls.

'I will not have my students treated this way. It's ridiculous, Mildred. How you keep that bully on your staff is quite beyond me. I've a good mind to call in the police.'

The girls knew they shouldn't be listening.

'Who do you think she's talking to?' Millie whispered.

'Someone called Mildred,' Sloane whispered back.

'Wow! You're a genius, Sloane.'

Sloane poked her tongue out at Millie.

Alice-Miranda turned to leave.

'Where are you going? I thought you wanted to see Miss Grimm,' Millie said.

'Yes, but she's busy and we'll have to come back later.'

From the other side of the wall there was another thump. 'Ophelia, Professor Crookston is the finest teacher in my school and I will not have you, or that child there, malign his good name. In fact, I will not have your children full stop, amen. I refuse to take any girls from the sixth grade into Sainsbury Palace next year or any year henceforth. They are nothing but trouble – just look at that Goldsworthy brat. The father said that he would build us a new library and all we got for our trouble was a half-done building and a pile of debt. The man should be in prison.'

'I believe that he is!' Ophelia Grimm shouted back. 'And I think you're being completely unreasonable. Your board of governors won't be impressed to hear that you've just tossed all those students. I don't know how you'll fill the spots at such late notice.'

'Well, unlike at this dump you call a school, I have a waiting list as long as your arm.' Mildred Jelly's voice was quivering now. 'So unless the girl is willing to apologise and retract her accusations, there is nothing else to discuss.'

'Mrs Jelly, I hardly think that is appropriate, given Mr Plumpton and a dozen other girls all witnessed exactly what went on. I can't blame Jacinta for standing up for herself – clearly the fire was nothing but an unfortunate accident caused by your staff member, who shouldn't have left a young student in charge of equipment she had no experience with.'

Outside the door, the three girls stood wide-eyed, wondering what was coming next.

Unfortunately it was Mildred Jelly. The study door flew open. Millie grabbed Alice-Miranda's hand and ducked behind a grandfather chair opposite Mrs Derby's desk. Sloane made a run for the hall and hid behind a potted palm. Mildred Jelly slammed the door behind her and huffed and blew all the way out of the office and up the corridor.

Alice-Miranda stood up.

'What are you doing?' Millie whispered.

'Going to see Miss Grimm. We have to tell her that we heard what happened.'

Millie shook her head. 'No we don't.'

Sloane reappeared. 'What's going on?'

'Alice-Miranda wants to tell Miss Grimm we heard everything,' Millie explained.

'Do you think that's wise?' Sloane asked. 'I can't believe Mrs Jelly has kicked them all out before they even started.'

'And where will they go?' Millie asked. 'I know my parents had me on the waiting list here and over there from the time I was born.'

Sloane shrugged. 'Well, I'm not going to just any old dodgy school. They'd better sort it out before the end of next year.'

Alice-Miranda frowned at Sloane. 'You said you didn't even know if you were booked in there in the first place. I'm sure it's just a misunderstanding.'

'I don't want to go there anyway,' said Millie.

'Alice-Miranda, Millie, Sloane, would you mind coming in here please?' Miss Grimm called from the other side of the wall.

Millie and Sloane jumped. 'Seriously that woman has superpowers,' Millie said.

Alice-Miranda led the way to the study door, knocked gently and pushed it open. Miss Grimm was sitting at her desk. 'Hello girls. Please come in.'

They were all surprised to see Jacinta sitting opposite the headmistress.

Alice-Miranda rushed to her side and gave her a hug. 'Oh Jacinta, are you all right? I've been so worried.'

Jacinta nodded.

'Miss Grimm, I'm very sorry, we didn't mean to hear what was happening in here. It's just that we came to look for Jacinta and then I was about to knock when we heard voices and it sounded like a bit of a row. Mrs Jelly wasn't very happy at all, was she? You're wonderful for standing up for Jacinta like that,' Alice-Miranda prattled.

'Let's sit over there.' Miss Grimm stood and beckoned for the girls to move to the couches in front of the fireplace.

'What's going to happen to the sixth-grade girls now?' Alice-Miranda asked.

The headmistress's lips drew into a thin line. 'I'm afraid I don't know. Perhaps Mrs Jelly will calm down but even if she does, I don't know if I want to send my girls there. I imagine I'll be making quite a few phone calls this afternoon to try to sort things out. In the meantime, I need all of you to keep this absolutely to yourselves. There is no point worrying the other girls and staff and I especially don't want parents to be concerned. This is my mess and I'll fix it.'

'Don't you mean it's *my* mess,' exclaimed Jacinta. Her eyes filled with tears. 'It's my fault that the girls are being punished and now they're going to hate me – just like they did before.'

'Oh, Jacinta, that's not true.' Alice-Miranda leaned in and put her arm around the girl.

'It sort of is,' Sloane said. 'Her fault, I mean. Not that they'll hate you. But they might.'

'Sloane!' Alice-Miranda and Millie chided.

'All right, they probably won't hate you but the parents will.'

Miss Grimm gave her a death stare. 'Sloane, I think it might be best if you kept quiet.'

Sloane gulped. She'd seen that look before and she didn't like it one little bit.

'Now, do I have your word that you will not discuss any of what you've just heard with anyone – staff, students or parents?' Miss Grimm looked meaningfully at each girl.

They all nodded. Millie's stomach let out a strangled whine. Her cheeks flushed the same colour as her hair. 'Sorry, Miss Grimm.'

'Right. Well, girls, lunch will be almost over and by the sound of it, Millie, you haven't yet eaten. Hurry along.'

Millie, Sloane and Jacinta filed out into Mrs Derby's office.

Alice-Miranda lingered a moment longer. She looked up at the headmistress. 'Miss Grimm, I have an idea.'

'Well, perhaps you should stay and tell me about it,' the headmistress said. Because at that moment she was at a complete loss.

Chapter 28

At the end of the school day, Alice-Miranda walked back to Grimthorpe House, where she bumped into Miss Reedy.

'Hello Alice-Miranda,' the English teacher greeted her. 'Did you have a good day?'

'Hello Miss Reedy. Yes, I think so.' Alice-Miranda half-smiled and half-frowned at the same time. 'What time do you want us at singing practice?'

'I'm afraid we've had to cancel. Mr Trout broke a tooth at lunchtime and he's got an emergency dental appointment. I need to be here, as we haven't got anyone to cover for Mrs Howard yet, so we'll catch up later in the week.'

'Is there any news on Mr Parker?' With all of the drama surrounding Jacinta and Mrs Jelly, Alice-Miranda had quite forgotten until then that there were search teams out looking for him.

The teacher shook her head. 'Charlie came in earlier and said that there was still no sign.'

'Seeing that our rehearsal is cancelled, could Millie and I go out on Bony and Chops again for a little while and help with the search?'

Miss Reedy looked at the clock. It was just after half past three. 'I don't see why not. Just be careful and make sure that you're back before dinner at six.'

'Thank you, Miss Reedy.' Alice-Miranda raced off down the hallway to get changed and see if Millie had already arrived back at the house.

Twenty minutes later the two girls were cantering across the open field towards the woods.

Millie turned in the saddle to face her friend. 'Where should we go?'

'What about the other side of the stream, further past Gertrude's Grove?' Alice-Miranda suggested.

'I've never been that far before,' Millie said. 'You don't think we could get lost, do you?'

Alice-Miranda shook her head. 'If we do, I just have to give Bony his head and he'll soon sniff out the nearest vegetable patch around – and surely there would be a house with a telephone close by.'

Millie nodded. 'Okay, lead the way.'

Alice-Miranda squeezed Bonaparte's flank and the pony loped along. When the pair reached the edge of the woods, Alice-Miranda pulled gently on the reins and he slowed to a trot. Fortunately she was so small in the saddle that the overhanging branches didn't present any real danger. The girls rode across the meadow known as Gertrude's Grove.

Instead of tying the ponies up along the fence as they often did, Alice-Miranda opened the gate that led to the stream and they continued on their way. They found an old path and rode deeper into the woods.

'It's a bit creepy in here,' Millie said, turning her head to look around. She was almost expecting a witch to fly out of the undergrowth. 'You know, if we'd mever met Miss Hephzibah and we still believed in the legend of the witch in the woods, I'd be terrified right now.'

'I'm sure there's nothing to worry about, Millie,' the child replied. 'Mr Parker,' she called into the foliage. Millie did the same.

The track broadened and Alice-Miranda glimpsed a flash of red in the distance.

'Can you see that, Millie?' A small red sedan was parked further along on the edge of the track, partly hidden by some overhanging branches.

'I wonder who owns it,' said Millie.

Alice-Miranda shrugged. 'I don't know but I think Bony needs a drink and there's a stream just down there.'

She slid from the saddle, took the reins over his neck and walked towards an old timber bridge.

Millie did the same. 'I don't think anyone's been across that for a while,' she said, after noticing the missing timbers and disintegrating posts.

The girls walked the ponies down a rough path to the edge of the stream, where Bony and Chops plunged their lips into the cool flowing water and slurped loudly.

Bonaparte pulled his head up and whinnied, spraying water all over Alice-Miranda.

'You horrid monster,' she said, laughing as she wiped the slime from her cheek.

But something had upset the little horse. He swivelled around and seemed transfixed on a large oak tree behind them.

'What is it, boy? What can you see?' Alice-Miranda held his reins tightly.

There was a rustling sound and Alice-Miranda spotted Bony's target. 'Millie, there's someone up there.'

Millie could see the figure high above them now too. 'That's a bit weird.'

'Let's go and say hello.' Alice-Miranda pulled on Bonaparte's reins and walked him back up onto the gravel track. An old fence lined the way and although it was a bit shambolic, there was an upright section just perfect for hitching the ponies to.

'Hello,' Alice-Miranda called. 'Are you all right up there?'

The figure moved and Alice-Miranda saw that it was a woman.

'Hello,' the woman replied.

'We're looking for someone,' Alice-Miranda said. 'You haven't seen an old man out here, have you?'

The woman shook her head and began to make her way out of the tree. She used the branches like steps and in a few seconds had leapt from the lowest limb onto the ground.

Alice-Miranda noticed that she was very tall and slim and had pretty red curls tied back in a ponytail. She thought she looked about the same age as her Aunt Charlotte.

'My name is Alice-Miranda Highton-Smith-Kennington-Jones and I'm very pleased to meet you.' The child held out her tiny hand.

The woman smiled and took Alice-Miranda's hand into her own.

Alice-Miranda noticed that she had a pair of binoculars slung around her neck. 'Are you looking for Mr Parker too?'

'Mr Parker?' The woman frowned and shook her head. 'Why? What's happened to him?'

Alice-Miranda launched into the story of Mr Parker's accident and recent awakening. The woman looked taken aback.

'Do you know Mr Parker?' Alice-Miranda asked as she finished her tale.

The woman shook her head. 'No. Not at all. But that's an awful story.'

'I'm Millie,' the red-haired child spoke up.

'Sorry Millie, it was terribly rude of me not to introduce you,' said Alice-Miranda.

'Hello,' the woman replied.

'You didn't tell us your name,' Alice-Miranda reminded her.

'It's Ursula.'

'If you're not helping search for Mr Parker, then may I ask what you were doing up that tree?' Alice-Miranda asked.

'Oh . . . just work.'

'What sort of work do you do?' Alice-Miranda asked.

'Are you a spy or a secret agent or something?' Millie added.

Ursula's eyes twinkled. 'I'm a secretary.'

'A secretary?' Millie frowned. 'Why would a secretary be up a tree with a pair of binoculars? I thought secretaries worked in offices.'

Ursula grinned. 'I do. It's just that I'm helping my boss on a special assignment.'

'Who's your boss?' Millie asked.

'You certainly ask a lot of questions, don't you?' Ursula replied. 'His name's Silas.'

'What a strange coincidence,' Alice-Miranda said. 'We met a man called Silas just yesterday, at Miss Hephzibah's. He's the mayor and he had got lost while looking for something out here and

Miss Henrietta had given him a cup of tea and some directions.'

Ursula's mouth twitched into a nervous smile.

'Is he your boss?' Millie asked.

The woman nodded slightly. She could hardly believe that these girls were the two children Silas had mentioned in his tale.

'The world really is the smallest place, isn't it?' Alice-Miranda beamed. 'Did Mayor Wiley find what he was looking for?'

'Yes, I think so, and quite a bit more actually.'

'We did too,' Millie said with a large grin. Alice-Miranda nudged her sharply in the ribs.

'Millie, you know we promised not to talk about that.'

'Do you mean the gold in the cave?' Ursula asked.

Millie and Alice-Miranda looked at each other, their eyes wide.

'But we didn't tell Mayor Wiley about that,' Millie said. 'We only talked to Miss Hephzibah and Miss Henrietta and we promised to keep it a secret.'

Ursula sighed. Silas had neglected to mention that he hadn't actually been told about the gold. Eavesdropping was one of his specialities and clearly he'd been doing a great job of it yesterday.

'I'm afraid that my boss has a rather big set of ears on him,' Ursula said.

'Was Mayor Wiley planning to tell anyone else about our discovery?' Alice-Miranda's forehead wrinkled into a deep frown.

'Yes,' Ursula replied. 'I think so.'

'But Miss Hephzibah and Miss Henrietta said that it would be better for everyone if it stayed a secret. We need to talk to Mayor Wiley right away,' Alice-Miranda declared.

'I suspect it could be too late for that,' Ursula said.

'Excuse me for saying this, Miss Ursula, but considering he's your boss and you said that you were here to help him with a special assignment, you don't sound as though you're very happy about whatever he's doing,' Alice-Miranda observed.

'I'm not, actually. That awful woman's plans are a travesty. I can't stand that he's helping her,' Ursula replied.

'Which awful woman?' Alice-Miranda asked.

'Finley Spencer. She's after the woods for a housing estate and now that Silas knows about the gold, I'm afraid that the development will go from bad to worse. It's terrible enough to think of all this beautiful land covered in brick veneer boxes, but imagine if she decides to build a goldmine instead!'

'Where exactly was Mayor Wiley going yesterday, before his detour to Caledonia Manor?' Millie asked.

'He was trying to find the owner of the land to convince them to sell,' Ursula said. 'He's hoping for a big fat commission.'

'Who owns the land?' Alice-Miranda asked.

'An old fellow,' Ursula replied, her voice wavering slightly.

'But Finley Spencer can't *make* him sell his land,' Millie said.

Alice-Miranda frowned. 'That's true, Millie. But I think the law's different when it comes to who owns things like gold or silver, because it's not *on* the land but *in* the land,' the child said. 'I was reading about it when we did an assignment in Science last term. It's very complicated. Someone can register a claim for the mining rights even if they don't own the land.'

Millie sighed and smiled at her friend. 'Trust you to know these things.'

'Why don't we go and find the man who lives out here and warn him about Ms Spencer's plan?'

Alice-Miranda looked at Ursula. 'Do you know his name?'

The woman nodded. 'Mr Frost.'

'Do you know where the house is?' Alice-Miranda asked.

'It can't be over there.' Millie pointed at the dilapidated bridge. 'No one's driven over that in years by the look of it.'

'I think it is,' Ursula replied. She'd been wondering about the state of the bridge herself.

'Really?' Alice-Miranda said. 'Have you been out here before?'

Ursula shook her head. 'No, I just looked up some old maps . . . at the council. The house is about a mile from the stream.'

Millie looked at her watch. 'We need to be back on time or Miss Reedy will have a fit.'

Alice-Miranda frowned. 'I'm sure she won't, not if she knows that we're on important business. Were you planning to go and see him?' she asked Ursula.

The woman looked surprised, as if she hadn't thought of that at all.

'No . . . I was just going to leave this in the letterbox at the end of the road.' She reached into her jacket pocket and pulled out a white envelope.

'We could take it to him,' Millie offered. 'It won't take long to get there on Bony and Chops and we can still get back to school in time.'

Alice-Miranda nodded. She'd been thinking the exact same thing.

'Miss Ursula, excuse me for asking, but is there a reason you didn't walk to the house yourself?' Alice-Miranda asked. She wondered what the woman was really doing. If she only meant to leave the letter in the letterbox at the end of the road, why was she up the tree with a pair of binoculars?

'Dogs,' Ursula replied. 'I'm terrified of them.'

'Dogs?' Millie frowned. 'Has Mr Frost got vicious dogs?' She wasn't too keen about going there herself if that was the case.

'I don't know but I'm such a wimp I wasn't willing to risk it,' Ursula replied.

Alice-Miranda wasn't convinced. She was sure there was something Ursula wasn't telling them.

'We'd better get going, Alice-Miranda,' Millie said.

Alice-Miranda looked at the letter. 'Shall I take that then?'

'Oh, yes please.' Ursula handed it to her.

'And don't worry – we won't tell him where it came from.'

Ursula frowned.

'I'm sure that your boss wouldn't be very happy if he found out you'd warned Mr Frost about his and Ms Spencer's plan,' Alice-Miranda explained. 'I had assumed the note was anonymous.'

'Oh, of course.' A look of relief passed across the woman's face. 'I'd appreciate that very much.'

Alice-Miranda and Millie walked over to the ponies and were mounted and ready to leave in seconds.

'It was lovely to meet you, Miss Ursula,' Alice-Miranda called.

Millie waved as she urged Chops forward. 'Goodbye.'

Ursula waved back. 'Thank you, girls. And please be careful crossing that stream.'

'We're fine,' Millie turned and called back. 'It doesn't look too deep.'

'I suppose it's not,' Ursula said. She turned to walk back to her car. 'Just promise you won't ever try when it's raining,' she muttered under her breath.

Chapter 29

Alice-Miranda and Millie crossed the stream and cantered along the track.

Millie urged Chops to go faster. 'We'd better hurry up. Let's just give him the letter and get back.' She wasn't looking forward to riding home through the woods at all.

A few minutes later the trees thinned and the cottage hove into view.

'My goodness, what a pretty little place,' Alice-Miranda exclaimed. 'You'd never know it was out here.'

'Someone must spend a lot of time in that garden.' Millie pointed beyond the low stone wall that surrounded the front of the house.

The sound of barking dogs caused Millie to tug sharply on Chops's reins.

Two cocker spaniels, one tan and one black, raced around the side of the building, their stumpy tails quivering.

'It's all right, Millie. I don't think we're in any danger of being eaten by these two.' Alice-Miranda slid out of the saddle and pulled the reins over Bony's head. 'Hello there.' Alice-Miranda bent down to pat the furry beasts who danced around her. 'Aren't you the cutest little things?'

'Maudie, Itch, what is it now?' a man's voice called.

Alice-Miranda stood up as a fellow wearing khaki overalls and a checked shirt appeared. He had a thatch of grey hair and a stout shape about him.

He stiffened when he saw the girls and their ponies.

'Hello there,' said Alice-Miranda. 'You must be Mr Frost.'

She walked towards the man with Bony clip-clopping behind. Millie slipped down from Chops's back and caught up to her friend.

'Hello there yourself,' he said, wondering how she knew his name.

'My name is Alice-Miranda Highton-Smith-Kennington-Jones. I'm very pleased to meet you, Mr Frost.'

The man hesitated then took her tiny hand into his.

'It is Mr Frost, isn't it?' she asked.

'Yes, Stan Frost. But how did you know?'

'A friend told us,' Alice-Miranda replied vaguely.

'I'm Millie.' The other girl held out her hand. Stan Frost shook it as well.

'To what do I owe this visit, girls?'

'We wanted to give you this.' Alice-Miranda retrieved the envelope from inside her jacket pocket and handed it over.

Stan Frost peered at it. 'Who sent you?' he asked suspiciously. He was wondering to what levels that development company would stoop to get hold of his land. Sending children on horseback was a bit desperate.

'A friend,' Alice-Miranda replied.

'Mmm, I see,' Stan scoffed. 'And how much are they paying you to try to convince me to sell?'

'Oh, that's not it, Mr Frost. We're not here for Ms Spencer. Quite the opposite.'

Stan Frost frowned. None of this was making much sense at all.

Bonaparte began to paw at the ground. Suddenly he let out an explosive whinny and tugged sharply on the reins. 'Oh, no you don't.' Alice-Miranda pulled hard. She looked around urgently. 'Mr Frost, do you have a vegetable patch?'

'Yes, just around the back of the cottage.'

'I'm afraid we'd better be going then,' she replied. 'My Bonaparte has a habit of getting into trouble whenever there are vegetables on offer.'

The pony was becoming more and more agitated.

'I think he'd have trouble getting into my patch,' Stan Frost replied. 'It's Cynthia, Cherry and Pickles proof.'

'Who are they?' Millie asked.

On cue, Cynthia began hee-hawing with all her might. Stan grinned. 'That donkey knows when she's being spoken of.'

'You have a donkey?' Millie smiled. 'I love donkeys. What about Cherry and Pickles, are they donkeys too?'

'Goats,' said Stan.

'As much as I'd like to meet them, I think we should get going.' Alice-Miranda was struggling with Bonaparte, who was throwing his head up and down. She pulled the reins back over his head and hauled herself into the saddle. Millie did the same.

Just as she wheeled the naughty Bony around, Alice-Miranda remembered something else. Since meeting Ursula she'd been so busy thinking about Mayor Wiley and Finley Spencer that she had almost forgotten the reason she and Millie had been out riding in the first place.

'Mr Frost, there is one other thing. Before we offered to deliver your letter, Millie and I were looking for someone.'

The back door banged and Maudie and Itch took off towards the noise.

'Stan, do you want me to peel some potatoes?' a deep voice called.

'I'm coming in,' Stan called back.

'Who's that?' Millie asked, thinking that if it was Mrs Frost she had an awfully manly tone.

'Who is it you're looking for?' Stan Frost asked.

'Mr Parker,' Alice-Miranda replied. 'Mr Reginald Parker.'

The owner of the deep voice appeared.

Stan Frost turned and looked at his friend.

Alice-Miranda studied the second man's face. 'Mr Parker, it's you! You're alive!'

Reg Parker wondered who the child on the shiny black pony was and why she was so excited. 'Of course I am,' he said, frowning. 'Do I know you?'

'Sort of,' Alice-Miranda replied. 'Mr Frost, this is such good news. We need to telephone Constable Derby right away.'

Reg Parker's forehead wrinkled. 'What's he got to do with anything?'

Stan ignored him and said, 'I'm afraid my telephone's not connected.'

'Goodness, I imagine that explains a lot,' Alice-Miranda said.

Stan Frost looked at Alice-Miranda and Millie. 'How about you girls ride around to the field. We'll put those ponies in with Cynthia for a minute so you can come inside. I think we need to talk.'

Chapter 30

Alice-Miranda and Millie led the ponies around to the other side of the cottage and into the field with Cynthia and the goats. They hitched the reins into the bridles, pushed up the stirrups on the saddles and let Bony and Chops run loose. The enclosure wasn't terribly big and Mr Frost said that he had an excellent supply of carrots to entice the pair back to the fence.

Cynthia seemed very pleased with her equine company and greeted Bony and Chops with a chorus of strangled hee-haws. They both seemed a little wary of her and ran off to the other side of the field with the donkey in hot pursuit.

'She looks like she's laughing and trying to tell a story all at the same time,' Millie observed.

'She's a good old girl,' Stan smiled. 'Keeps me company.'

The children followed Mr Frost to the house. Mr Parker had already retreated back inside to get some drinks. He didn't have a clue what was going on.

Stan Frost turned and looked at the girls. 'I'm very glad that you found us. I knew that something wasn't quite right with old Reg but he's been a closed shop since he arrived.'

'Not like his wife,' Millie replied.

'You can say that again,' Stan agreed. 'But she's gone now, hasn't she?'

'Gone?' Millie frowned. 'Where?'

'Reg told me she'd gone so I assumed he meant she was gone the same as my Beryl,' Stan replied.

Alice-Miranda realised that Mr Frost was saying his wife had died. She shook her head. 'No. Mrs Parker's alive and well and worried sick about Mr Parker.'

'Oh,' Stan exhaled loudly. 'Dear me. Poor old

Myrtle. Who'd have thought I'd ever say that?' He shook his head.

'How long has Mr Parker been here?' Alice-Miranda asked.

'He walked across the field out of the blue on Saturday afternoon. You could have knocked me down with a feather. I haven't seen him for . . .'

Millie ended the sentence. 'Three years?'

'Yes, that's right. When I asked him where he'd been all this time he said that he was here yesterday, which had me a little confused. Do you know what happened to him?'

'Mr Parker had an accident. He was cleaning out the gutters and fell off the roof. He bumped his head and broke his leg but he should have been fine – except that he fell into a coma and he's been asleep in the sitting room for the past three years,' Alice-Miranda explained.

Stan Frost's eyes widened. 'Are you sure?'

'Oh yes, quite sure. Millie and I have seen him at home and I've been reading to him once a week. We'd all been hoping that he'd wake up soon. You can imagine poor Mrs Parker's shock when she came home from doing the shopping and he was gone,' the child added.

'But surely she didn't just go out and leave him on his own?' Stan asked.

'No, of course not. Mr Parker's had a nurse looking after him but she was gone too so everyone assumed that they had disappeared together,' Millie explained.

'Reg run off with the nurse! I can imagine how well that went down with Myrtle.' The old man grinned.

'All the evidence seemed to point that way to begin with but then Alice-Miranda found a note among the washing and we learnt that he hadn't gone with Nurse Raylene at all. There are search parties out looking for him today,' Millie said.

'Well, come on, let's get inside and see what he has to say for himself.' Stan ushered the girls through the back door.

They removed their boots and followed Mr Frost through a small hall into the country kitchen. Four tall glasses sat on the round table and Reg Parker placed a jug of cordial in the middle. There was a plate of digestive biscuits beside it.

'I wondered if you were still coming,' said Reg, arching an eyebrow at Stan.

'I was just introducing the girls to Cynthia,' Stan

replied. 'And they were filling me in on a few things. I think we need to get you home, Reg.'

Reg began to pour the drinks. 'I told you before, I've got nothing to go home to.'

'Oh, Mr Parker, that's not true. Mrs Parker is so worried about you. She'll be beside herself when she finds out that you're alive,' Alice-Miranda said.

'But she's gone,' Reg replied.

'Mr Parker, why don't you sit down and I'll finish that,' the child said soothingly. She took the jug and began to fill the cups.

Reg looked at her and wondered why there was something familiar about that voice. 'Do I know you?'

'I've been reading to you, Mr Parker. We've shared some lovely stories. I thought you were going to wake up when we got to the part in *Matilda* where she glued her father's hat to his head. It's very funny and I could have sworn you almost smiled.'

A glimmer of recognition passed across his face.

'Do you remember something?' she asked, looking at him closely.

'I don't know,' Reg replied. 'Just a strange feeling.'

'I get those all the time,' Alice-Miranda said. 'You should listen to them.'

'She's right, you know,' Millie agreed.

Alice-Miranda finished pouring the drinks and set the jug down. Then she sat in the spare seat opposite Mr Parker. She wanted to break the news to the man as gently as possible. 'Mr Parker, you don't know this, but until Saturday you'd been asleep for three years.'

'That's ridiculous!' he retorted.

'It's true, Mr Parker,' said Millie. 'You had an accident and fell off the roof one afternoon. The doctors said that you should make a full recovery but then one day you fell asleep. You'd been that way ever since, until you woke up and walked off.'

'I think it could be true, Reg,' said Stan Frost, nodding. 'I told you I hadn't seen you in three years and you insisted you'd been here the day before. But I can tell you that's not the case at all.'

'Well, if you haven't seen me for three years, how come you didn't know what happened to me? I thought we were friends,' Reg said.

'I called your house loads of times and got no answer. Then one day, about a month after I'd last seen you, Myrtle picked up and she said you weren't talking to anyone. I thought you'd dumped me. You know how Beryl felt about our friendship too.

When you didn't come back out here again she told me that Myrtle had probably found out where you were going every day and put a stop to it. I wanted to come and find you but Beryl was a strong woman, Reg. She thought it was best for everyone if I just let things lie.' A wry smile perched on the man's lips as he finished speaking.

'What are you smiling about, Stan?' Reg demanded. 'If any of this nonsense is true then I don't think it's very funny.'

Millie smiled too. 'He said "let things lie" and that's what you were doing.'

But Reg still couldn't see the funny side of it.

'Then Beryl got sick, and I don't know . . . It was just easier to be by myself,' Stan gulped.

'Mr Parker, we need to get back to school but as soon as we do, I'll telephone Constable Derby. I'm sure he'll arrange for someone to come and collect you,' Alice-Miranda said.

Reg picked up a biscuit. 'But I don't think I want to go back.'

'With all due respect, Mr Parker, Mrs Parker is quite lost without you and she'll be so relieved to have you home again. And I'm sure the doctors will want to give you a full check-up. It's a miracle that you've woken up after all this time,' said Alice-Miranda seriously.

'I suppose it might explain a few things I've been wondering about. Like why I'm so slow and what these marks are on my wrist. And I've been ravenously hungry ever since I got here too. But I don't want to see Myrtle,' Reginald replied, shaking his head slowly.

Millie and Alice-Miranda exchanged curious looks.

'But she's your wife,' Millie said.

'And if I remember anything about her,' Reginald said, cradling his chin in his hand, 'her list of chores for me won't have got any shorter over the past three years.'

'You're right about that,' Stan muttered.

'But you have to go home. Mrs Parker will be heartbroken,' Alice-Miranda implored him.

Reginald shook his head. 'No. I won't go. No one can make me.'

'Can we at least let Constable Derby know where you are so they can call off the search?' Alice-Miranda asked. 'It would be very unfair to keep people out looking for you when you're quite safe and well here.'

Reginald bit his lip and frowned. 'I suppose that's for the best, but you tell that young whippersnapper that he's not to let Myrtle know where I am. You tell her that I will come home when I'm ready.'

'If you really want it that way, Mr Parker, of course it's up to you. But I think it's awful to make Mrs Parker suffer a minute longer,' Alice-Miranda reluctantly agreed.

'That's the way I want it,' Reginald said firmly.

Stan Frost remembered the envelope that the child handed him. He'd put it into his overalls pocket.

A strange silence shrouded the group. Alice-Miranda glanced around at the room. There were a few photographs, mostly of Mr Frost and the lady she assumed was his wife. There was another with two children.

Stan pulled out the letter and scanned the page.

Dear Mr Frost,

I regret to inform you that your property is under threat from Finley Spencer, who has recently been advised by Silas Wiley that there may be a deposit of gold to be found in the caves on the ridge. In the name of saving the woods and surrounding areas of natural beauty from destruction on a catastrophic scale, I recommend that you register a claim immediately and refuse any offers to purchase the land.'

Yours,
A friend

Stan Frost's jaw dropped. 'Where did this come from?' He turned the paper over in his hand and looked for any indication of a name. 'And how in God's name did this Finley Spencer person find out about the gold?'

Reginald Parker sputtered his tea all over the table. 'But we're the only ones who know about that.'

'We promised not to tell, Mr Frost,' Alice-Miranda said.

'She didn't want you to know,' Millie added.

'She?' Stan asked.

'Urs–' Millie stopped and coughed loudly.

Stan and Reg looked at each other. 'Ursula?' they said in unison.

'Is that what you were going to say?' Stan whispered.

Millie shook her head.

Alice-Miranda decided that they'd better come clean. After all, the woman was only trying to help. 'Well, yes, that is her name. But you mustn't tell anyone because she would be in terrible trouble with her boss if he found out that she had warned you about Ms Spencer's and Mr Wiley's plans.'

'How old is the woman?' Stan Frost asked.

'I'm not entirely sure, Mr Frost. You know it's impolite to ask a lady her age but if I were making a guess I'd say around her mid-thirties.'

'She has red curls,' Millie said.

'Red, you say?'

'Yes,' Millie replied. 'She's very pretty. Why? Do you know her?'

Stan shook his head. 'No, I don't think so.'

Reg shook his head too.

But Alice-Miranda wasn't so sure. She was now quite convinced that there was something Mr Frost and Mr Parker weren't telling.

Reginald sighed. 'I told you, Stan, you should have registered that claim years ago. Now, how do you intend to do it – seeing that your car doesn't run, your bridge is broken and the telephone's been cut off?'

Stan Frost was wondering that himself. 'Hang about, Reg. We've never actually found much gold up there, other than those few old rocks years ago. Why does this Silas fellow think that the caves are some sort of Aladdin's Treasure?'

Alice-Miranda and Millie glanced at each other across the table.

'We found a cave up on the ridge too,' Millie began. 'Well, Alice-Miranda found it. The hole was so small I didn't even think we'd get inside but we did.'

There was a pause.

Reginald stared at Millie. 'Well, what did you find?'

Alice-Miranda continued the story. 'The cave was all sparkly and pretty. It looked like it was sprinkled with fairy dust. Millie and I were just looking about, when I followed an especially bright line. We could hardly believe it when the line turned into what appeared to be a seam of gold.'

'I told you there was gold up there,' Reginald crowed, turning to look at Stan. 'That's what I dreamt. But it wasn't our cave.'

'When we told Miss Hephzibah and Miss Henrietta about the gold, they said that it would be best for everyone if we kept it to ourselves but Mr Wiley must have overheard our conversation and now he's going to tell Finley Spencer and I'm afraid that with all the might of her company behind her, we could be powerless to stop her,' Alice-Miranda explained.

'But you have to stop her,' Reginald insisted. 'Stan and I have only been looking for fun, but if someone as powerful as you say this Finley woman is gets hold of the news, she'll destroy the woods and the ridge and everything else around here. If she gets the rights to mine the land, Stan's farm will be nothing more than a giant hole in the ground. We never wanted that.'

Stan Frost bit his lip. 'There's got to be a way to save Wood End.'

Alice-Miranda was thinking.

Millie glanced at the kitchen clock. It was after five and the girls had promised to be back before dinner. 'We have to get going, Alice-Miranda.'

The child nodded. 'Mr Frost, you said that you wouldn't tell anyone about the gold even if you'd discovered it.' She looked at him expectantly.

Stan nodded.

'Do you have any children?' Alice-Miranda asked.

Stan Frost looked at Reg. His eyes filled with tears. 'I had a son and a daughter. But they're gone now.' He ran a hand over his face.

'I'm so sorry to hear that, Mr Frost.' Alice-Miranda reached across and patted the old man on the forearm. 'Have you thought about what you're going to do with Wood End in the future?'

Stan frowned. 'The future?'

'When you retire. Were you planning to sell up and travel the world, perhaps?'

'Heavens, no. I've already retired and I was planning to spend the rest of my life right here, tending my garden and looking after the animals. I have no desire to be anywhere but here for the rest of my days,' the old man replied.

Alice-Miranda nodded. 'Well, that's wonderful.'

'I don't see how it's wonderful if some rotten woman is going to turn my farm into a ruddy great goldmine,' said Stan.

'What are you thinking?' Millie asked.

'I don't really know yet,' Alice-Miranda replied. But she had an idea. It was just a matter of finding out whether or not there was a chance it could work.

The girls bade farewell to Mr Frost and Mr Parker, vowing to be back as soon as they could with any news.

It didn't take long to entice Bony and Chops to the fence with a couple of fat carrots. Sadly, they were both too slow and Cynthia managed to snatch both of the juicy vegetables before they took a bite. She hee-hawed loudly, then took off at a speedy trot around the field with Cherry and Pickles in hot pursuit.

'She's a character,' Alice-Miranda laughed. She gave Bony a pat while Mr Frost walked over to the vegetable patch and pulled some more carrots for the ponies.

'She's a hairy monster,' said Stan. He thrust the carrot in Bony's direction. The pony quickly demolished it in two bites.

Reginald Parker was standing nearby, fidgeting. 'Now, promise you won't tell Myrtle where I am.'

'Of course, Mr Parker, if that's what you really want,' Alice-Miranda reassured him.

'I'd appreciate it.' The old man's face creased into gentle folds as he smiled at the two girls. 'I'm not saying I never want to see her again. I'm just not ready yet.'

'Hopefully soon,' Millie said. 'Mrs Parker's been very upset, especially when she thought you'd run off with Nurse Raylene.'

'Run off with the nurse?' Reginald's brow wrinkled.

'I'm afraid so,' Millie nodded.

'She's lost her marbles for sure. Only woman I've ever loved is Myrtle. I just need a few days.'

The two girls mounted their ponies. Dark clouds had gathered while they'd been inside and it had now started to rain.

'Goodbye Mr Frost,' Alice-Miranda called. 'Goodbye Mr Parker. It really is wonderful to finally meet you.'

Millie said goodbye and waved at the gentlemen as the ponies began to trot down the driveway towards the stream.

'What lovely little girls,' Stan said as he led Reg back inside the house. He felt a pang of regret, like a punch to his stomach.

'That Alice-Miranda's a real card, you know,' Reg replied. 'That story she was reading . . .' He stopped and stared at Stan. 'How did I remember that?'

'I don't know but I think we'd better get you to that doctor sooner rather than later,' Stan replied.

Chapter 31

Alice-Miranda and Millie cantered towards the school, eager to get back before dinner. The black sky had made good its promise and the girls and their ponies were now soaked to the skin. They arrived at the stables sodden and completely out of breath.

'We're never going to make it in time,' Millie puffed as she looked up at the stable clock. 'We'll have to get changed before dinner too. Miss Reedy will murder us.'

Elsa, the new stablehand, appeared from inside one of the boxes.

'Hello girls – oh, look at you two. I was wondering how much longer you'd be out,' she said with a smile.

'Hello Elsa,' said Alice-Miranda. She removed her helmet and began to unbuckle Bony's girth straps. 'We hadn't planned to be quite so long but we met some friends and got a little bit sidetracked.'

'You'll both catch a death of cold in those wet clothes! I can put these two away,' Elsa offered.

'Thanks, Elsa, that's fab,' said Millie.

'Be a good boy for Elsa,' whispered Alice-Miranda to Bony. She blew gently into his nostrils. The little pony snorted and Alice-Miranda wiped a small amount of slime from her forehead. 'What will I do with you?' she giggled.

Millie gave Chops a quick pat too.

'You'd better get moving,' said Elsa. 'Susannah was up here earlier and she said that Miss Reedy was on the warpath down there.'

'Thanks, Elsa. I promise we don't usually do this,' Alice-Miranda called as she and Millie charged out into the pouring rain and down the driveway towards the boarding house.

They almost bumped into Miss Reedy, who was hiding under a large umbrella on her way to dinner.

'Girls, look at you. I thought you'd be back at least half an hour ago,' she scolded them. Miss Reedy was surprised to see the girls and realised that she'd failed to make sure that everyone had returned to the house before dinner. She wasn't enjoying her dual role and couldn't wait for Mrs Howard to get back.

'Miss Reedy, we have some wonderful news,' Alice-Miranda blurted.

The teacher frowned. 'It had better be good. You'll need to get out of those clothes before dinner.' She turned and walked back up the path and opened the door to Grimthorpe House. Once inside, Miss Reedy went ahead and found a couple of towels that Mrs Howard always left in a little cupboard in the sitting room in case of such emergencies.

The teacher wrapped a towel around Millie and then Alice-Miranda.

'We found Mr Parker,' Millie blurted, unable to wait any longer.

'And he's absolutely fine,' Alice-Miranda added.

'Goodness, really?' Miss Reedy's eyes were wide. 'That's wonderful news. Where is he?'

Alice-Miranda and Millie told her all about meeting Ursula and Mr Frost and then finding Mr Parker.

No one had noticed Jacinta standing in the hallway. She'd been in her room and wondered why the house had fallen silent when she realised that she was late for dinner. Not that she felt like eating. She was still churned up about the meeting with Mrs Jelly and the news that none of the girls would be attending Sainsbury Palace because of her. She'd expected Miss Grimm to be furious, but she wasn't – at least, not about what happened at the orientation. Jacinta had still been in trouble for her late-night escape to the stables and had received a solid telling-off for her moody behaviour, but that was hardly anything really.

She'd been about to head off to the dining room when she heard voices and realised that Miss Reedy was in the back sitting room with Alice-Miranda and Millie.

Jacinta couldn't believe her ears. Mr Parker had been found! He was alive and well and this was her chance to do something good. She'd telephone her mother right away. Mrs Parker would be so grateful.

Jacinta poked her head around the doorway and spied the telephone sitting in its cradle just inside the room. She reached around and picked it up, then sped silently to her bedroom and quietly closed the door.

'Mummy,' she whispered down the line. 'I have some wonderful news. You must tell Mrs Parker right away.'

Back in the sitting room, the girls and Miss Reedy were discussing what to do next.

'We have to call Mrs Parker at once,' Miss Reedy said. 'She'll be so relieved.'

'That's what we said, but I'm afraid you can't,' said Alice-Miranda.

'I don't understand,' Miss Reedy said. 'Of course we have to let the poor woman know.'

'Mr Parker made us promise that we wouldn't tell her where he is. He said that he's not ready to go home yet,' Alice-Miranda explained.

'Poor man.' Miss Reedy shook her head. 'It sounds like he's in shock. I don't think he knows what's good for him at all.'

Miss Reedy stood up. 'I'll call Constable Derby and he can decide what's best.' She walked towards the telephone and was surprised to see it missing.

She pursed her lips. 'That's strange. I could have sworn it was right there a moment ago.'

She walked into Mrs Howard's office, wondering if she'd put the handset down in there and forgotten about it. A quick scan revealed nothing.

'One of the girls must have taken the phone to her room,' she murmured as she walked back into the sitting room. 'I've told them before that's not on. You two run along and get changed and I'll keep looking for the phone.'

The two girls raced down the hall. Jacinta heard the footsteps and told her mother that she had to go.

Miss Reedy strode from room to room checking for the missing telephone. She was stunned when she opened Jacinta's bedroom door to find the girl lying on her bed, headphones in and reading a book.

'What are you doing here?' Miss Reedy shouted.

Jacinta pulled out the earphones and frowned at the teacher.

'Is it dinner?' she asked innocently.

'Yes, fifteen minutes ago.'

'I didn't hear the bell,' Jacinta replied with a shrug.

'Well, you can get going over there right now,' the teacher said. 'And have you seen the house phone?'

Jacinta shook her head.

Miss Reedy spun around and caught sight of the handset poking out from under a pile of papers on Sloane's desk.

'I've told Sloane Sykes before that she doesn't have sole rights to the telephone!' Miss Reedy snatched it up and stalked out of the room.

Jacinta shuffled off her bed and slipped on her loafers before following Miss Reedy down the corridor.

Back in the office, Miss Reedy telephoned Constable Derby, who was relieved and amazed to hear her news.

Chapter 32

Ambrosia Headlington-Bear had been busy trying to finish her article outlining clothing and packing tips for an island holiday when Jacinta called. She'd been hoping to get it finished that evening – it shouldn't have been difficult, given she'd been on so many tropical getaways over the past few years. But those days were gone – there was no money for research at the moment. Ambrosia wondered how Myrtle Parker would react to the good news. She pulled on her boots, threw on a coat and snatched up an umbrella.

Across the road, she could see a light on in Myrtle's sitting room. She skipped up the porch stairs and rang the bell.

Inside, Myrtle Parker was in the middle of dusting. She'd spent all day looking for Reginald, driving up and down the lanes and searching the sheds at the showground. But there had been no sign. She was quite convinced that he had relapsed somewhere in a field. Silly man, whatever had possessed him to get up and leave? And where on earth did he think he was going? At least he'd had the wherewithal to put on some clothes, which Myrtle had discovered when she'd found his blue striped pyjamas in the load of washing Alice-Miranda had put on the day before.

The old woman looked up at Newton the gnome, who was sitting quietly on the mantelpiece taking it all in.

'Did he say anything to you?' she asked the concrete creature. 'Suppose not.' Myrtle flicked the duster over the gnome's head and sighed. The sound of the doorbell startled her and she almost sent the little fellow flying. He wobbled and then thudded back into position.

'What is it now?' Myrtle huffed under her breath. She bustled to the door and wrenched it open.

'Hello Myrtle,' said Ambrosia. 'I have some news.' She closed her umbrella and forced her way inside the front hall.

Myrtle tutted. She hadn't even invited the woman in.

'I think you should sit down,' Ambrosia instructed and ushered Myrtle into the sitting room.

The old woman pursed her lips. 'And I think you should take that wet coat off. I don't need you dripping all over my lovely floors.'

Ambrosia did her best not to roll her eyes, and tugged at the sleeves on her coat.

The old woman lowered herself onto the sofa. She felt a twinge in her stomach.

'Well, what is it? I haven't got all night, you know. Some of us have work to do.' She flicked the feather duster into the air.

Ambrosia reached out and placed her hand onto Myrtle's. 'I've just got off the phone with Jacinta and she said that she knows where Reginald is.'

Myrtle Parker swallowed and looked at the woman. 'Well, where is he? And how does she know? Did she see him?'

Ambrosia shook her head. 'No, I don't believe so.'

'You're not going to tell me some gobbledegook

about the child having telepathic powers are you?' Myrtle said dubiously. The past few days had been like riding a roller-coaster and she didn't think she could stand another free fall.

'He's with some fellow called Stan out in the woods, at a place called Wood End,' Ambrosia replied.

Myrtle said nothing but her face turned a horrible shade of grey.

'Are you all right?' Ambrosia asked. 'Isn't it wonderful news? Mr Parker will be home with you in no time.'

'I should have known,' Myrtle whispered.

'Why should you have known?' Ambrosia asked. 'Who is this Stan fellow?'

Myrtle Parker stood up. She strode into the kitchen and gathered up her handbag and car keys. She then disappeared into the bedroom and jammed her pillbox hat onto her head, then stopped at the hall mirror to check that it was straight.

'Are you coming?' she called to Ambrosia, who was wondering if Myrtle was having some kind of breakdown. Her behaviour was often curious but this was strange, even for her.

Ambrosia scurried to the front hall. 'Are you going to find him?'

'Yes. If it's the last thing I do,' Myrtle replied. 'Now, are you coming with me or do I have to undertake this mission alone?'

There was no way Ambrosia was going to let Myrtle Parker out on her own. Not in her current state and in this weather.

'Of course,' Ambrosia replied. For the second time in two days, she found herself heading out with her neighbour. At least this time they knew where they were going.

'Well hurry up. We haven't got all night.'

'Mr Parker will be so glad to see you,' Ambrosia said as the two women hopped into Myrtle's little hatchback.

But Myrtle didn't reply. She was thinking about what she would say to Reginald when she found him.

Chapter 33

Constable Derby had called off the search for Mr Parker immediately after he'd hung up on his call with Miss Reedy. He was relieved to hear that the man was alive and well and staying at Wood End with Stanley Frost. He hadn't been out to that part of the world in years and didn't know that Stan still lived there, so this was very good news. He was less relieved to learn that Mr Parker didn't want anyone to tell Mrs Parker where he was just yet. He could only imagine how she'd take it.

The constable was about to drive around to see Myrtle when a crackly call came through on the radio. There'd been a serious accident on the road between Downsfordvale and Winchesterfield. He'd have to attend that first and then go to see Mrs Parker.

Constable Derby kissed his wife goodbye, pulled on his raincoat and hurried out into the darkness. A brisk wind had sprung up and the rain was coming in sideways. He hated bleak nights like these. They only ever brought trouble. There was more news of the accident over the radio. A lorry loaded with glass bottles of tomato sauce had overturned on a bend and was now blocking the road in both directions. The driver had escaped with only minor cuts and there were no other vehicles involved, but it sounded like he would be needed there for hours.

The police car sped through the rain, siren blaring. As he rounded the bend, Constable Derby sighed at the scene in front of him. The truck was wedged between the stone walls that lined the carriageway. They'd need a crane to lift it back onto its wheels and some manpower to clear up the debris before the road was safe to use again. He called over to the Downsfordvale station for backup but it seemed that everyone there was already out on calls too. Apparently a fire had started in one of the local restaurants and there had been another accident in the village. For the moment Constable Derby was on his own and it looked like it would be a very long night.

☆

Myrtle Parker's hatchback zoomed on into the darkness, windscreen wipers going full tilt but barely making an impression on the screeds of water washing over the car.

Ambrosia Headlington-Bear was beginning to think it would have been better to take her convertible, given it was almost brand new and far better equipped than Myrtle's old banger.

'Myrtle, where is Wood End?' Ambrosia asked as they passed the showground. 'And who's Stan Frost?'

But Myrtle was concentrating on the road. The little car hit a huge puddle and veered violently to the left. Ambrosia screamed and somehow Myrtle regained control of the vehicle.

'Probably best you focus on the driving,' said Ambrosia. 'We can talk about Mr Frost later.' She smiled nervously at the old woman and wondered if there would be a later.

Myrtle Parker's face looked as if it were set in concrete; her steely gaze was fixed on the road and her hands clamped tightly to the steering wheel.

Further along, Myrtle slowed down and seemed to be looking for a place to turn. Ambrosia couldn't see anything resembling a road and was stunned when the old woman steered the car into what looked like a thicket of bushes. The little hatchback bumped along the track under a deluge of overhanging branches.

Ambrosia nibbled nervously on her thumbnail. 'Are you sure this is the way?'

Myrtle nodded. 'Oh yes, I'm quite sure.'

The thwacking branches clawed at the car as Myrtle planted her foot on the accelerator. The vehicle fishtailed from side to side and bounced along the pitted track.

'Look out!' Ambrosia's hands covered her eyes. She peeked just in time to see Myrtle avoid hitting a large branch that came crashing down onto the path behind them.

'Perhaps we should come back tomorrow, when the weather's cleared,' Ambrosia said tentatively. But she wondered if they would be able to turn back now anyway.

Myrtle shook her head. 'I'm taking Reginald home with me tonight if it's the last thing I do.'

Ambrosia was beginning to think that it could very well be the last thing that either of them did.

The path opened up a little. Water was sheeting across the windscreen and visibility was almost nothing. Up ahead, she could just make out what looked like an old bridge.

'Myrtle, stop!' Ambrosia demanded.

But the car sped up.

'Stop being such a baby, Ambrosia.' Myrtle glanced at her, brows furrowed. 'This bridge is as safe as houses.'

As the little hatchback's front wheels hit the structure, it disintegrated beneath them. A wave of water from the swollen stream rose up and swept the car away. The younger woman's screams filled the vehicle as it spun around and around. Myrtle was silent, her face stony, her hands still gripping the steering wheel.

The car raced downstream in the torrent of swirling water.

'I don't want to die,' Ambrosia wailed. 'I've got Jacinta to think about.'

Myrtle glanced at her hysterical friend. 'I am sorry, dear. I didn't mean for this to happen.'

The next moment, the world turned black for both of them.

Chapter 34

Millie and Alice-Miranda lined up at the servery in the dining room. They had walked over from the house with Miss Reedy, who said that Constable Derby had been delighted to hear that Mr Parker had been found. He had agreed not to tell Mrs Parker of her husband's whereabouts just yet either. The teacher and girls decided it would be best to keep the good news to themselves until Constable Derby had been out to Wood End.

Millie raised her nose in the air. 'I think Mrs

Smith has outdone herself tonight. I love lamb korma.'

'Me too,' said Alice-Miranda as she dropped an extra dollop of yoghurt onto her meal.

Jacinta was sitting in the corner with Sloane.

'How are you feeling?' said Alice-Miranda as she set her plate down beside Jacinta's.

'I'm fine,' said the girl.

'What did you talk to Miss Grimm about after we left?' Sloane asked Alice-Miranda.

'I can't say. I'm sorry, but I promised I wouldn't tell. Miss Grimm said that we shouldn't get anyone's hopes up.'

Millie had meant to ask Alice-Miranda about that too, but in all the excitement of finding Mr Parker, she'd completely forgotten. Now she pulled a pleading face at her friend. 'Come on, Alice-Miranda, we're your best friends.'

'I know you are and that's why I can't tell. Not yet,' Alice-Miranda said. She looked at her plate pointedly and took a bite of her meal. 'Mrs Smith's a genius with curry, isn't she?'

Millie got the hint. 'She's got a lot better this year. This tastes like something we had at your place, Alice-Miranda.'

The girl nodded. 'I think it's another one of Mrs Oliver's recipes.'

Sloane shovelled a forkful into her mouth. 'It's pretty good. My mother is the worst cook in the world. I'm going to starve this summer. I bet she'll be on some new diet that she'll inflict on the rest of us. Last year it was disgusting cabbage soup morning, noon and night.'

'Oh, that's seriously gross,' Millie agreed. 'Cabbage makes me windier than a summer storm.'

The other girls giggled.

Sloane grimaced. 'There were some smells in our house that no one should ever be subjected to.'

'It's sad that we'll all be split up for the holidays,' said Alice-Miranda, frowning. 'What does everyone have planned?'

Millie piped up first. 'We're going to stay in the caravan by the beach. Mummy said that you can all come, as long as you don't mind sleeping on camp beds and roughing it a bit.'

'I'd love to,' said Alice-Miranda. 'But I'll have to check what Mummy and Daddy have planned. I think I might be staying with Granny for a little while too.'

Sloane, however, had been shaking her head in horror. 'No way. I'm allergic to camping.'

'You can't be *allergic* to camping,' Millie protested.

'Well, I am,' Sloane insisted. 'Just the thought of sleeping in a tent can give me hives, and with skin as delicate as mine I can't afford to risk it.'

'You're so pathetic.' Millie wrinkled her nose at Sloane, whose tongue shot out at her.

Jacinta stayed quiet.

'What about you, Jacinta?' Millie asked.

The girl shrugged. Her dark mood seemed to have returned.

'Come on, Jacinta, it's only camping. It wouldn't kill you,' said Millie.

'I don't care what I do for the holidays. When my father finds out what's happened, he'll probably send me to some boot camp for brats in the middle of nowhere so I can't get into any more trouble.'

'Oh, Jacinta, I'm sure that won't happen,' Alice-Miranda told her friend.

'Stop being so nice to me. I don't deserve it.' Jacinta pushed her chair out, picked up her plate and walked over to deposit it on the servery.

Alice-Miranda wondered what else to say, because at the moment nothing seemed right at all.

☆

Silas Wiley sat at his kitchen table reading through the paperwork. He couldn't believe how easy it was to register the claim. Thankfully, the fees could be paid by credit card, although he'd had to use his mayoral expense account, which he'd reimburse as soon as he could. It wasn't ideal but Ursula would know how to work things out at the end of the month. She was a clever girl.

Now it was just a matter of waiting for the official documentation and then he could bring in the workers – although he needed to figure out who those workers would be. This wasn't going to be any amateur prospecting outfit. Silas envisaged a full-scale mining operation. And he wanted one of those giant trucks and a processing plant too, where he could watch all that beautiful molten gold being poured into bars. Registering the claim was one thing; now he had to find people who knew what to do with it.

He went to the dresser where his parents had always kept the telephone books. He didn't have a computer at home and this couldn't wait until tomorrow. Surely he could find someone who would assist him with his mission – although mine managers were probably a little thin on the ground.

There was the small issue of money too. Until the mine was showing a profit, Silas would have to cut someone in on the deal, because there was no money for up-front payments.

He tapped his pen on a blank piece of paper and thought about who might need to be involved in a mining venture.

Surveyors. He'd need to get a survey. Flipping through the pages, Silas found what he was looking for and wrote down a couple of numbers. He picked up the telephone and dialled.

Chapter 35

Constable Derby finally returned to the station at quarter to four the next morning. The accident had taken hours to clear up and it was now far too late to go and see Mrs Parker. His visit would have to wait a little while; at least until he had a shower and a couple of hours' sleep. The rain was still coming down, but it was nothing like the tempest that had made the night so wretched.

Several hours later, he struggled out of bed and drove around to Rosebud Lane. It was just after seven o'clock when he rang Myrtle Parker's doorbell. To his astonishment, the front door was ajar. He poked his head inside.

'Mrs Parker, are you here?' The young man edged inside and scanned the front hall. It didn't look as if anything was missing. He walked into the sitting room and thought it was much as he remembered it.

A quick sweep of the house revealed nothing, although he couldn't see Mrs Parker's handbag or keys anywhere and the little hatchback was missing from its usual spot on the driveway. It was certainly curious.

The constable decided to see if Mrs Headlington-Bear knew where Myrtle might be. He approached the pretty white cottage and knocked on the door. Nothing. On his way to try the back door, he peered in through one of the windows. The room clearly belonged to Ambrosia, but the bed was made and there was no sign of anyone.

The constable got back into his car, threw his sodden hat onto the passenger seat and turned the ignition. There would be no point heading for Wood End just yet – the stream would be flooded for sure. Livinia Reedy and her charges were next on his list. Alice-Miranda and Millie had found Mr Parker, so it was important to interview them – and at least he knew exactly where to find them.

☆

Alice-Miranda and Millie were on their way to breakfast, trying to keep dry under their umbrellas, when they spotted the police car coming up the driveway.

'Good morning, constable,' Alice-Miranda called as the policeman hopped out of the vehicle and headed towards them.

'Morning girls, I was hoping to catch you before school.'

'Are you all right?' Millie said urgently and pointed at his jacket sleeve. It was covered in what looked like thick red blood.

Constable Derby glanced at his arm. He raised it and sniffed, then wiped a smidge of the substance onto his finger and licked it. 'Just the leftovers from last night's accident.'

Alice-Miranda and Millie's jaws dropped.

'Ewww, gross,' Millie gulped.

Constable Derby grinned. 'It's tomato sauce, girls. I thought you would have heard about the lorry crash.'

'We did,' Millie replied. 'But we didn't know what it was carrying and you've got to admit, that does look a lot like blood.'

'Sorry to scare you. It must be the lack of sleep,' the man smiled.

Alice-Miranda giggled.

'Could we talk somewhere private?' the constable asked.

Alice-Miranda nodded. 'We could go to Mrs Derby's office. She's not in yet, is she?'

'No, when I left home she was still in bed. Poor woman has had to put up with me coming and going at all hours, so I was pleased not to wake her.'

The trio scooted across the courtyard and into the school reception. Jacinta had spied the group too. She followed them to the main building and hid herself in the alcove just outside Mrs Derby's office door.

'Isn't it wonderful news about Mr Parker?' Alice-Miranda exclaimed.

'Yes, it certainly is,' the constable replied.

'How did Mrs Parker take the news that he's been found but isn't ready to come home?' Millie asked.

'I haven't told her yet. I was at the accident last night and I was the only man available. What with the wild weather, all the other officers from Downsfordvale were busy and, besides, I wanted to tell her myself. I've just been around there now but she's not home. I went to see if Mrs Headlington-Bear knew where Mrs Parker could be but she wasn't about either.'

'Have you visited Mr Parker?' Millie asked.

The constable shook his head. 'Afraid not. With all this rain, I wouldn't have a hope of getting across the stream out there at Wood End.'

Jacinta's stomach lurched.

'Did anyone else know about Mr Parker?' the constable asked.

'Just Miss Reedy and us,' Alice-Miranda informed him. 'I'm sure that Miss Reedy wouldn't have told anyone. She said that we should keep it secret until Mrs Parker knew and things were sorted out.'

Jacinta stepped around the corner into the room.

Millie jumped. 'Were you spying on us?'

The girl shook her head. 'No. But I think I've messed up. Again.'

Constable Derby frowned at her. 'Hello Jacinta. What's happened?'

'I told Mummy about Mr Parker and she was going to tell Mrs Parker.'

'But how did you know?' Alice-Miranda asked.

'I overheard you both telling Miss Reedy last night and I thought Mrs Parker would be so grateful to know,' Jacinta replied. 'I thought I was doing the right thing. Please believe me.'

'But we told Miss Reedy that Mr Parker wasn't ready to come home yet.' Millie's eyebrows knotted together fiercely.

'I didn't hear that part. I promise,' the girl pleaded.

'Oh dear.' The constable shook his head. 'Let's just hope that Mrs Parker and your mother didn't try to get to Wood End last night.'

Jacinta's eyes brimmed with tears. 'I'm sorry. I'm so sorry.'

Alice-Miranda put her arm around her friend. 'It's all right. I'm sure that they'll be fine.' Alice-Miranda was glad Jacinta couldn't see her face, because in truth she wasn't sure at all.

'I'll head out that way now,' the constable said. 'If your mother and Mrs Parker tried to get there last night, they're most likely bogged on the track somewhere.'

'We could go on the ponies,' Alice-Miranda offered. 'But we'd have to ask Miss Grimm.'

At that moment, the doors to Miss Grimm's study opened and the headmistress emerged.

'Good morning, Miss Grimm,' the group chorused.

'Hello everyone,' the headmistress said slowly, as she looked at her unexpected visitors. 'Why are you crying, Jacinta?'

Jacinta shook her head and remained silent.

Alice-Miranda launched into the story of how she and Millie had found Mr Parker. '. . . And now we think that Mrs Parker and Mrs Headlington-Bear might have tried to drive out there last night and perhaps they're stuck somewhere because of the rain,' the child finished.

'Do you think you can get there in the car, constable?' the headmistress asked.

'Only if they got no further than the creek near the showground. I heard over the radio that the road there is now blocked too,' the man replied.

The headmistress looked at Millie and Alice-Miranda. 'Do you think you can reach Wood End on your ponies?'

The two girls nodded. 'The rain seems to be easing off and we promise not to do anything silly,' Alice-Miranda reassured Miss Grimm.

The headmistress sighed. 'I'm not entirely comfortable with this.'

'Please, Miss Grimm, we'll be extra careful,' Alice-Miranda begged.

'All right, off you go then. And take this.' She picked up a two-way radio that Mrs Derby kept on her desk, which allowed her to communicate with Charlie Weatherly, the gardener.

'Actually, Alice-Miranda, give me that for a moment,' said Constable Derby. He fiddled with the dials and there was a blast of static. He winked. 'I've tuned it to my police radio frequency. Just for today.'

Miss Grimm smiled. She'd often wondered how Mrs Derby seemed to know what was going on around town well before anyone else did.

The two girls said goodbye and rushed off to the boarding house to get changed into their riding gear. Jacinta was about to skulk off too but Miss Grimm asked her to stay behind as there was something important she needed to discuss with her.

'I'll head off and see how far I can get on the road,' the constable promised. 'And don't worry, Jacinta. We'll find them.'

But Jacinta wasn't convinced. It was her news that had sent her mother and Mrs Parker out in the middle of a terrible night. If anything had happened, she would never forgive herself.

Chapter 36

The driving rain had eased to drizzle as the girls set off on Bony and Chops. The ground was sodden and slippery so they took the ride at a careful trot.

The creek at Gertrude's Grove was swollen, but judging by the flattened vegetation it had already gone down considerably from its peak.

The radio in Alice-Miranda's saddlebag crackled. Bonaparte skipped sideways, startled by the noise.

'It's all right, Bony, don't be scared,' the child soothed and gave him a reassuring pat. She pulled gently on the reins, then retrieved the radio from the bag.

'Alice-Miranda, are you there?' The constable's voice came through remarkably clearly.

She pushed the speaker button and said, 'Hello Constable Derby. Yes, we're here.'

'I've made it further than I expected to. I'm on the driveway at Wood End,' the man reported. 'There's a large tree down on the road. I'm going to keep coming on foot, so hopefully I'll meet you at the bridge shortly.'

'We're almost there,' Alice-Miranda informed him. 'See you soon.' She placed the radio back in the saddlebag.

'You forgot to say over and out,' Millie said, smiling.

Alice-Miranda grinned. 'Oops, I'm not very good with that sort of thing.'

Millie glanced around at the overhanging branches. Weighed down with water in the dull morning light, they looked more ghostly than ever. 'Come on, let's get moving. I hate these woods.' Millie urged Chops forward.

They trotted on and reached the crest where they had spotted Ursula's car the day before.

'Oh no!' Alice-Miranda gasped. The stream was raging and the bridge, which had been rickety to say the least, was now completely washed away. Worse still, there were muddy tyre tracks leading towards where it had been.

'Someone's been here,' Millie called over the rushing water. 'Do you think it could have been Mrs Parker and Mrs Headlington-Bear?'

Alice-Miranda shook her head. 'I hope not.'

'Look, over there!' Millie pointed.

Mr Frost and Mr Parker were walking down the track on the far side of the stream, with the two cocker spaniels beside them.

Alice-Miranda shouted, 'Mr Frost, Mr Parker, hello.' She waved her arms and Bonaparte whinnied.

Stan and Reg saw the girls.

'Hello there!' they called back.

Alice-Miranda pointed to the bridge. 'We think someone's tried to cross there last night.'

Stan Frost's eyes widened as he realised the bridge he had failed to maintain had been completely swept away. 'But the bridge is gone!'

Reg shook his head. 'They didn't have a hope of getting across there.' His eyes searched for tyre tracks on their side of the stream but the ground was clear.

'Do you know who it was?' Stan called back. He felt as if his stomach was lined with rocks. His mouth was parched and his breathing had become shallow. Terrible memories flashed through his mind. Not again. Surely they couldn't lose anyone else.

'We think it was Mrs Parker and our friend's mother, Mrs Headlington-Bear,' said Alice-Miranda. She hopped down from Bony's back and walked him as close to the water as she dared. Millie did the same. The tyre tracks led straight to the point where the bridge had been.

Reg Parker gulped and his lip began to quiver. 'Myrtle? My Myrtle? It's my fault. I should have gone home as soon as you lot told me what had happened. I'll never forgive myself if anything's happened to her.'

'We need to go that way,' Alice-Miranda called back, pointing at the torrent.

Stan nodded.

Alice-Miranda mounted Bony and the little pony spun around. She urged him forward, and with Millie and Chops close behind, began to walk downstream. The ponies could cover much more ground than the men on the other side and within a few minutes Mr Frost and Mr Parker were out of sight.

It was even more obvious now that the stream had been much higher during the night. There was debris strewn all around, which made it harder for the girls to pick their way along the bank.

'You should call Constable Derby,' Millie said.

Alice-Miranda nodded and pulled the radio out of her saddlebag. 'Constable Derby, come in.' She waited for him to reply. The static crackled. She spoke again but there was nothing.

'Come on, Millie, if Mrs Parker and Mrs Headlington-Bear were washed away there's still a chance they're all right. We need to find them, fast.'

Bonaparte began to snort. He whinnied loudly and pawed at the ground, refusing to go any further.

'What is it, Bony?' The child scanned the banks ahead of her but couldn't see anything. Bony threw his head up and down. Suddenly, Alice-Miranda saw it. 'Oh my goodness!' She dug her heels into the pony's flank and he charged forward, slipping sideways on the muddy bank.

'What is it?' Millie couldn't see anything out of the ordinary.

'Up there!' Alice-Miranda pointed into the trees. Firmly wedged in a giant V of an ancient oak tree was

Myrtle Parker's little red hatchback. 'Mrs Parker, Mrs Headlington-Bear, are you there?'

Inside the car, Ambrosia Headlington-Bear and Myrtle Parker had spent a very frightening and uncomfortable night waiting to be rescued. Both of them had been knocked out cold after their rollicking ride downstream. When Ambrosia regained consciousness she'd tried to open her door, and found that it was stuck fast. It wasn't until she looked out the window that she realised where they were. The revelation had caused Myrtle to faint as soon as she'd come to. After that, they'd both dozed on and off during the night. They stayed as still as possible, trying not to upset the balance of the car.

'Did you hear that, Myrtle?' Ambrosia wondered if her ears were playing tricks on her.

Myrtle stirred and slowly opened her eyes. 'What?'

'Someone's out there.' Ambrosia peered down and saw Alice-Miranda and Millie riding towards them. 'Help!' she shouted and wound down the window. At that moment she was quite glad that Myrtle's car was ancient and had old-fashioned window winders.

'Ambrosia's alive,' Millie called.

Both girls jumped off their ponies, tied them to a low branch and raced towards the car. It seemed to be stuck fast.

'Is Mrs Parker okay?' Alice-Miranda shouted.

Ambrosia stuck her head out of the window and nodded.

Alice-Miranda raced back and grabbed the two-way radio out of Bony's saddlebag, hoping it would work this time.

'Constable Derby, come in,' she urged. There was a loud crackle and the man's voice burst through the static.

'Hello, Alice-Miranda, where are you?'

'We've found them, and they're alive!'

'Thank heavens,' the constable sighed. 'Are they injured?'

'We can't tell,' Alice-Miranda said. 'They're up a tree.'

'Up a tree?'

'The car is and they're in it,' the child explained.

'How far past the bridge are you?' the man asked.

'Not too far. It was only a few minutes' ride.'

'Well, hold tight. I'll be there soon.'

On the other side of the stream, Mr Frost and Mr Parker came into view.

'They're up there!' Millie shouted.

The two men looked up and were stunned to see Myrtle's car balancing in the tree.

Reginald Parker was even more surprised when his wife's face appeared in the driver's window. His heart thumped and he began to cry.

'Oh, thank heavens.' Stan Frost's shoulders slumped and it looked as if the air had been sucked right out of him.

'Myrtle. My darling, Myrtle. Are you all right?' Reginald wailed.

Myrtle turned to Ambrosia. 'Look at him. Bawling like a baby.'

'Oh Myrtle, he looks sorry to me,' Ambrosia replied.

All at once Myrtle broke into shuddering sobs. She wound down the window and called, 'I love you, Reginald,' through a haze of tears.

Constable Derby reached the scene. 'Goodness, they really are up a creek, or should I say a tree, without a paddle,' he grinned.

'But at least they're alive,' said Alice-Miranda.

Chapter 37

'I still can't believe that you were up a tree, Mummy.' It was a week later, and Jacinta was helping her mother set the dining room table at Wisteria Cottage.

'I still can't believe we lived through it.' Ambrosia Headlington-Bear smiled at her daughter then walked back towards the kitchen. 'How are those pizzas coming along, Alice-Miranda?'

Alice-Miranda was busy spreading tomato paste onto a trio of pizza bases, while Millie and Sloane added the toppings.

'Very well, I think,' Alice-Miranda replied. 'Does Mrs Parker like pizza?'

'Everyone likes pizza, don't they? If she doesn't, there's salad and pasta,' Ambrosia replied, glancing at the clock. 'Speaking of salad . . .' She turned her attention to the lettuce sitting next to the sink.

After a long and involved rescue, Ambrosia and Myrtle had escaped their ordeal with nothing more than a few bumps and bruises. Myrtle and Reginald had a tearful reunion, during which he promised to come home and she promised to rein in her unwieldy lists. Reginald had spent a couple of days in hospital having a thorough check-up and was discharged with an extraordinarily good bill of health. His doctor planned to write up the case in a medical journal, which would no doubt attract further attention in the future. For now, Reginald asked that his story stay under wraps until he felt strong enough to speak with the press.

'Alice-Miranda, would you mind taking the salt and pepper shakers through to the dining room?' Ambrosia asked.

The girl nodded and disappeared up the hallway.

'Does this look okay?' Sloane pointed at the pizza she'd just topped with ham and pineapple.

'Ha,' Millie laughed. 'That looks like Mrs Parker.'

'Oh my goodness, Millie, I think you're right,' Ambrosia giggled. Sloane's decorating looked like a face, and it bore more than a passing resemblance to Myrtle.

'You can't leave it like that,' Millie admonished.

Ambrosia winked. 'Oh, I think you should, Sloane.'

In the dining room, Alice-Miranda placed the salt and pepper shakers on the table. 'I'm so glad you're feeling better, Jacinta.'

Her friend looked up. 'Thanks.'

The pair exchanged a secret smile.

The front doorbell rang, making both girls jump.

'Can you get that, Jacinta?' her mother called from the kitchen.

Jacinta walked down the hall and pulled open the front door.

Myrtle Parker was standing on the porch in a rose-patterned dress that made Jacinta's eyes hurt. Mr Parker was standing behind her.

'Hello Mrs Parker, Mr Parker.' She extended her arm, welcoming the couple inside.

'Good evening, Jacinta. Mmm, something smells good.' Myrtle raised her nose in the air then lowered her cheek, which Jacinta dutifully kissed.

'Hello Jacinta.' Reginald smiled nervously.

'Are you feeling better?' Jacinta asked.

Myrtle Parker tsked. 'Oh, I'm getting there, although I don't know if I'll ever recover from the shock of it all.'

Jacinta had been speaking to Mr Parker, who was about to say something but then thought better of it. The man winked at her and she winked back.

'Please come through into the sitting room. Mummy's in the kitchen with the girls,' Jacinta instructed.

'Hello Mrs Parker, Mr Parker.' Alice-Miranda bounded into the room and wrapped her arms around Myrtle's middle. She then did exactly the same to Mr Parker.

Myrtle smiled fondly at the girl. 'Now that's what I call a proper greeting.'

Jacinta rolled her eyes.

Ambrosia appeared and offered the guests something to drink.

The doorbell rang again. 'I'll get it,' Alice-Miranda said and raced off down the hall.

'Are you expecting anyone else?' Myrtle asked Ambrosia, who smiled benignly.

Ambrosia glanced at the dining room table

which had been set for nine. She frowned, wondering why there was an extra place setting. She knew of only one surprise guest.

Alice-Miranda returned to the sitting room with Stanley Frost in tow.

'What are you doing here?' Myrtle Parker demanded.

'I invited him,' said Alice-Miranda.

Reginald Parker stood up and shook hands with Stanley.

'But how did you get here?' Myrtle asked.

'Someone arranged for the young constable to come and collect me,' said Stan, smiling at Alice-Miranda.

'And how are you getting home again?'

'I think Mr Frost might need to stay over,' Alice-Miranda answered on his behalf.

'What about the animals?' Reg asked.

'I've got them sorted. They'll survive until I get back there in the morning,' Stan replied.

'Well, there's no room at our place.' Myrtle shook her head then caught sight of her husband, who raised an eyebrow. Myrtle had an apparent change of heart. 'Of course you're welcome, Stanley.'

'Oh Myrtle, I've missed you.' Stan walked towards the woman and planted a kiss on her powdery cheek.

Myrtle pursed her lips. 'I can't exactly say the feeling's mutual.'

But that wasn't true at all. She and her brother-in-law had once been close, until she fell out spectacularly with her sister Beryl. Beryl and Stan had a beautiful son and daughter, until a terrible tragedy had taken the boy from them. He'd drowned in the flooded stream when he and his sister had been out playing one afternoon. The girl had tried in vain to save him but he was lost. From then on, Beryl could only ever see the poor girl's faults. Myrtle had argued with her sister – she couldn't understand how Beryl could be so cruel. When Beryl had cut contact with the girl, Myrtle couldn't forgive her. Her own, longed-for children had never arrived and now the niece she had adored was allowed to disappear from their lives too. Myrtle had tried to keep in touch but the letters had stopped coming. She hadn't heard a thing in years.

'Well, it seems everyone knows each other,' said Ambrosia. She took Stan's drinks order and hurried off to the kitchen.

'Dinner won't be long,' Alice-Miranda informed the guests. She and Jacinta left the trio to talk and went back to the kitchen, where Millie and Sloane were putting the finishing touches to dinner.

The doorbell rang again. Ambrosia looked at Alice-Miranda.

'I'm afraid this one's a surprise,' the child said. 'I hope you don't mind.'

Ambrosia shook her head. 'What are you up to, young lady?'

'Who is it?' Millie asked.

'Just wait and see.' Alice-Miranda hurried off to greet their additional guest.

When she took Ursula through to the sitting room, Myrtle, Stan and Reginald were deep in conversation and didn't even notice the arrival.

Alice-Miranda coughed and said, 'Hello everyone, I'd like you to meet –'

'Ursula, is it really you?' Stan Frost stood up slowly. He stared at the young woman, wondering if she was a dream.

'Hello Dad,' Ursula said.

'But how?'

'You can thank this little one for convincing me to come tonight,' she said, flashing a smile at Alice-Miranda. She turned to the other guests. 'Hello Aunty Myrtle, Uncle Reg. I hear you've had quite the adventure over the past few days – or maybe that's years for you, Uncle Reg.'

'Oh, Ursula, darling.' Myrtle walked over to the woman and embraced her tightly. 'We've missed you so much.'

'And I've missed you too, Aunty Myrtle,' Ursula said. 'I just hadn't realise how much until recently.'

'But how do you know each other?' Stan looked at Alice-Miranda and then at his daughter.

'Millie and I ran into Ursula just before we met you at the farm the other day, and something didn't add up,' explained Alice-Miranda. 'Then you and Mr Parker both said her name together and denied knowing her. But in the house, there was a photograph. The girl in the picture had to be her – except for the blonde hair, and everyone knows that's easy enough to change.'

Ursula took up the tale. 'I went out to Wood End to warn you about that ridiculous boss of mine and that awful property developer. When I met Alice-Miranda and Millie they offered to take the letter to you. A couple of days later, I got a call at the council chambers from this little one.' Ursula glanced at her tiny partner in crime, her eyes glistening. 'She told me about everything that had happened: Of course I read in the paper about Aunty Myrtle being washed away just like Peter, and Alice-Miranda had explained about Uncle Reg being in a coma when I met her and Millie near the bridge. I heard that Mum had died from my charming boss. I guess it was the push I needed to see you. Life's too short. Whatever differences we had, Dad, I'm sure we can put aside for the sake of family.'

'Oh, Ursula.' The old man hugged his daughter fiercely. 'I'm so sorry. I tried – I sent you letters but they were all returned and I had to keep it a secret from your mother. Your mum was just such a strong woman. And after everything that happened, well, I was a weak, pathetic excuse for a father.'

'Yes, you can say that again,' Myrtle sniped.

Reg glared at his wife, who noticed his steely gaze.

'But then again, none of us are perfect, are we?' she added.

Stan and Reg exchanged curious glances then grinned. Coming from Myrtle Parker, that was surely the admission of the century.

'It was my fault too, Dad. I couldn't stay still, and for a long time I didn't want you to find me. When I came back here I wasn't sure that you'd want to see me anyway.'

'Of course I do, Ursula. I love you. You're my daughter.' Tears ran down Stan's cheeks. He mopped them with his handkerchief.

Millie, Sloane, Jacinta and Ambrosia carried the food from the kitchen into the dining room next door.

Ambrosia poked her head into the sitting room. 'Is everyone ready to eat? Oh, hello there.'

'I'm Ursula,' the younger woman introduced herself with a sniff. 'Sorry about crashing your party. I'm afraid it's all a bit emotional in here at the moment.'

'No, not at all. I can't wait to hear about whatever it is that's been going on.'

Millie's head popped out from behind Ambrosia. 'Hello Ursula, I didn't know you were coming.'

'Until a little while ago, I wasn't sure I was either,' Ursula replied with a smile.

The group took their seats at the dining table and within a few minutes everyone was enjoying the feast. When Myrtle commented on the delicious ham and pineapple pizza, Millie and Sloane grinned at each other.

'Have you heard any more about that Finley Spencer woman?' Reginald asked Ursula.

'Yes, she's decided not to go ahead with the development,' Ursula replied.

'Well, that's a relief, Stan,' said Reginald.

'I thought so too, until this afternoon. Silas Wiley told me that he was planning to make a big announcement to the press tomorrow. I asked him what it was about and he said it was a surprise. I have a terrible feeling it has something to do with Wood End,' the woman explained. 'Although he was blustering about not being able to get anyone to come to the council chambers for his press conference.'

'You *did* register that claim, didn't you, Stan?' Reg asked.

The old man gulped and slowly shook his head. With everything that had happened in the last week, it had completely slipped his mind.

'Stan! You're done for now.' Reg shook his head. 'You can kiss your lovely little patch goodbye and there'll be no more fun for us either.'

Myrtle Parker wondered what on earth they were talking about. Jacinta, Sloane and Ambrosia were in the dark too.

'Tomorrow must be the day for announcements,' Jacinta said.

Everyone turned and looked at her.

'Miss Grimm's making a big announcement tomorrow morning too. Remember, that's why we have to go back to school tonight?' she explained.

Ursula's brow creased. 'That's a coincidence. Silas is meeting the press at the school.'

'Maybe he's just coming along to support Miss Grimm,' Jacinta said with a shrug. 'Don't mayors like to get photographed for the paper?'

'Silas Wiley certainly does,' Ursula muttered.

But Alice-Miranda was convinced there was more to it than that. She climbed out of her chair. 'Excuse me, Mrs Headlington-Bear, may I use the telephone?'

'Of course,' the woman replied. 'Is everything all right?'

'Yes, I just need to make a quick call.' Alice-Miranda skittered out of the room.

'Whatever is that child up to now?' Myrtle Parker smacked her lips together noisily.

Chapter 38

'Good morning, everyone.' Ophelia Grimm stood centre stage in the assembly hall the following morning. 'I'm sorry to have dragged you away from your Saturday activities but I have a very important announcement to make and I wanted you all to hear it at the same time.'

At the side of the hall, several local newspaper reporters and photographers had gathered and the local radio journalist was crouched down in front of the lectern, pushing his fluffy microphone towards the headmistress.

Alice-Miranda, Jacinta, Millie and Sloane were sitting together in the audience.

'What are Miss Hephzibah and Miss Henrietta doing here?' Millie whispered. The two elderly women had been escorted onto the stage by Charlie Weatherly and were now seated at the end of the teachers' row, smiling at the girls.

Sloane shrugged. 'It must be something to do with the teaching college. I can't believe we're missing a game for this.'

Miss Grimm was about to speak, when she was distracted by someone entering the hall.

'Hello, hello girls, lovely to be here on this special day!' Silas Wiley strode down the centre aisle, his robes flowing and chain jangling.

'Seriously, what's he doing here?' one journalist asked another.

'I've never known anyone so keen to get his face in the paper,' said the other, shaking his head. 'And the robes? Again? You've got to be kidding me.'

Silas smiled at the cameras as he trotted towards the stage.

'Mayor Wiley,' Ophelia Grimm frowned. 'This is an unexpected surprise. What an honour to have you with us.'

Alice-Miranda felt her heart beat faster.

Silas strode across the stage and shook hands with Miss Grimm. 'Carry on, Miss Grimm. But I'd like some time after you, if I may?' Silas grinned at her and, after the teachers and guests had shuffled down, took a seat.

The headmistress shot the man a sidelong glance then continued her announcement. 'Girls, as you all know, quite a few months ago now, Professor Winterbottom and I made plans with Miss Fayle and Mrs Sykes to open a teaching college as part of the renovation of Caledonia Manor. Unfortunately, we have had no end of problems with some of the planning permissions with the council.' She turned and glared at Silas Wiley, who tried not to squirm under her gaze. 'So, I am afraid to say that the current project has now been put on hold.'

'Boring, who cares?' Sloane grouched.

The photographers snapped away, mostly in a bid to capture the sour look on Silas's face.

'But I have some good news. Many years ago, Caledonia Manor served as the original site of the Fayle School for Boys. As such, we have been able to employ a loophole,' Miss Grimm went on.

Jacinta reached out and grabbed Alice-Miranda's hand. Alice-Miranda smiled at her friend.

'I'm delighted to announce that we will extend Winchesterfield-Downsfordvale all the way through to leaving. As of next year, we will be a primary *and* secondary academy.'

The whole hall erupted with cheers.

'We can stay!' Susannah leapt into the air and hugged Ashima. Danika, the Head Prefect, jumped up from her seat on stage and hugged Miss Reedy.

Sloane's jaw dropped. Millie's did the same.

Alice-Miranda and Jacinta hugged each other tightly.

'You *knew.*' Millie's eyes were wide as she looked at her friends.

Alice-Miranda nodded. 'But we couldn't tell. Miss Hephzibah thought that Caledonia Manor had been used as a school once before, but she had to find the documents to prove it. We all hoped they hadn't been burned in the fire. Turns out they were in Professor Winterbottom's office over at Fayle. He remembered finding them when he made the changes to the charter earlier in the year.'

Jacinta leaned around and smiled at her friend. 'Your mother's meddling actually did some good, Sloane.'

'This is the best news ever,' Sloane blurted.

'Girls, please calm down,' Miss Grimm commanded.

Danika raced forward, leaned into the microphone and shouted, 'Three cheers for Miss Grimm.'

The girls responded and Miss Grimm took a step back. She waited for the cheering to die down and tried again.

'Girls, there are a few people to thank for this development. Miss Hephzibah and Miss Henrietta, who have so kindly agreed to make use of their beautiful house in this way; Professor Winterbottom, who helped us with the details; and Alice-Miranda, who first came to me with the idea.'

'What about Jacinta?' Sloane called.

'Yes, Jacinta Headlington-Bear, we have you to thank too. If you hadn't got into trouble over at Sainsbury Palace, I might never have known the truth about several things, nor had the gumption to do what I should have done years ago.'

Silas Wiley was growing impatient. The journalists all had their hands up eager to ask questions and the flashes were going off like fireworks.

He stood up and walked to the podium. Alice-Miranda watched him and tapped her fingers anxiously on her lap.

Millie looked over at her. 'Are you all right?'

'Fine,' the tiny child answered. But Millie wasn't so sure.

'Yes, yes, lovely news,' Silas said as he shoved Miss Grimm to one side. 'And I'm so glad that the council has been able to work with you to make things happen so quickly.'

'The council had nothing to do with it,' Sloane yelled.

Silas ignored her. 'Now, I'd like to make an announcement too, if I may.'

His next words were completely drowned out by the sound of a helicopter overhead. He waited a minute, expecting the noise to abate, but it only intensified.

Finally the racket stopped. Silas opened his mouth for another attempt, but the whole school suddenly rose to its feet.

'Girls, please, you don't have to stand on my account.' But they hadn't. Silas turned around to see what they were looking at. 'Your Majesty!' he croaked.

Queen Georgiana strode towards the lectern, nodding at Miss Grimm, who curtseyed back. Her lady-in-waiting, Mrs Marmalade, and bodyguard, Dalton, hovered at the edge of the stage.

'Good morning, everyone,' Queen Georgiana boomed into the microphone.

The girls chorused 'good morning' back.

'What's she doing here?' Sloane whispered.

Alice-Miranda finally felt as if she could breathe again.

Millie frowned at her friend, wondering what she'd been up to this time.

'Please be seated. I was staying at Chesterfield Downs and couldn't resist being here this morning to celebrate some very good news. Of course, I am as thrilled as you are about Winchesterfield-Downsfordvale continuing to leaving. I wish that had been the case when my granddaughters were here.'

Livinia Reedy shuddered. She was very glad that hadn't been the case at all.

'And now I know that Mayor Wiley has some very good news to share with you as well.' She smiled at Silas, who had retreated to his seat. He wondered how on earth she knew, but he was almost bursting inside that the Queen herself had chosen to come and applaud his entrepreneurial flair.

'Why don't you come up here?' Queen Georgiana turned to the man, who was relishing every moment.

Silas stood up and strode towards the lectern, jangling like a key chain. Who would have thought he'd be sharing the podium with the Queen?

'Mayor Wiley, I think one of the hallmarks of your time in office will be your generosity to the community,' she began.

Silas grinned like a shark.

'I know that you would love to have made this announcement yourself, given that the land in question falls into your council region, but I'm afraid I would like to honour the man myself, if I may?'

This wasn't what Silas was expecting to hear. He suddenly had a sinking feeling that the announcement she was about to make didn't involve his hundred-year mining lease.

'Just this week, I have learned that a very generous member of our community, Mr Stanley Frost, has decided to give his magnificent property, known as Wood End, to the Queen's Preservation Trust.' Queen Georgiana glanced towards Silas.

He almost choked.

'Of course, Mr Frost and any descendants of the family will retain the right to live in the cottage and use the land for their own purposes. I know that Mr Frost has always given you girls access to enjoy the woods and this will simply protect the area from greedy developers and other invasive ventures, such as – perish the thought –' Queen Georgiana turned to Silas Wiley and raised her eyebrows '– mining.'

The girls clapped loudly. Millie whistled until Miss Grimm cast an evil stare in her direction.

Silas couldn't believe his ears. 'But I have a claim,' he murmured. 'And a licence.'

'Afraid not, Mr Wiley. The only one who can issue that is me, and you'd be getting that land over my dead body,' Queen Georgiana whispered back.

Silas Wiley hadn't noticed Ursula and her father standing at the back of the room. They'd crept in earlier.

'I'm proud of you, Dad,' said Ursula. She squeezed her father's hand.

Alice-Miranda spotted the pair. She leapt from her seat and called, 'Mr Frost's here.'

'Oh, lovely.' Queen Georgiana peered out into the audience. 'Mr Frost, would you like to come up, please?'

Stanley Frost, supported by his daughter, made his way to the stage.

'Ursula?' Silas blurted. 'What on earth?'

'Thank you, Mr Frost.' Queen Georgiana shook the old man's hand.

'But, but!' Silas spluttered.

'Come now, Mayor Wiley, I've just made you a hero, when you could so easily have been the villain,' Queen Georgiana hissed through gritted teeth as she stood beside Stanley Frost and his daughter. Silas gulped and shuffled in between them as the cameras flashed.

'Thank you, Your Majesty,' Stanley smiled. 'And thank you to that little one out there, who came up with the idea in the first place.'

Queen Georgiana winked at Alice-Miranda, who winked right back.

And just in case you're wondering . . .

Jacinta finally confessed to Alice-Miranda, Sloane and Millie that she'd been so upset about the thought of leaving Winchesterfield-Downsfordvale that she decided to get into trouble on purpose so that Miss Grimm would make her repeat. She apologised for being a terrible brat and said that she had no idea her behaviour would cause such a huge fuss. As Sloane pointed out, in the end things had worked out for the best. Millie, however, couldn't resist telling Jacinta that there'd been no need to be such a pain about it all.

On hearing the news about Winchesterfield-Downsfordvale's progression into secondary school, Mildred Jelly had called and begged Miss Grimm to reconsider her decision. Apparently her long waiting lists were a figment of an overactive imagination. With every single girl making the decision to stay put, it wasn't long before an advertisement appeared in the paper for a new headmistress and Science teacher at Sainsbury Palace.

Ursula resigned from her position at the council. She couldn't stand to work for Silas Wiley a minute longer. As chance would have it, Miss Grimm advertised a casual position as a housemistress the very next day. Ursula is currently looking after the girls until Mrs Howard returns. After that, who knows. She and her father are taking things one day at a time.

Queen Georgiana arranged to rebuild the bridge across the stream and fix Stanley Frost's driveway. He had the telephone reconnected and Ursula insisted that he buy himself a new second-hand car.

Myrtle Parker agreed that Stan and Reg could continue their fossicking whenever they wanted. She put away her lists too and was stunned when Reg arrived home one afternoon with two plane tickets to Tuscany.

Nurse Raylene returned to Winchesterfield and was surprised to find herself out of a job. Her father had made a full recovery and she was thrilled that Mr Parker had too. Myrtle Parker was still quite glad to see her go – she was far too young and attractive to spend any more time than necessary with her Reginald.

Alice-Miranda and Mr Parker struck up a lovely friendship. She still went to read to him as often as she could, and together they shared books and poems and lots of laughs. He especially loved *Matilda*.

Silas Wiley's announcement with Queen Georgiana garnered him a great deal of support throughout the district. His entrepreneurial skills were still questionable, though; he decided to sell his pizza restaurant and invest in a putt putt golf course instead. He was devastated to lose Ursula, who had been the best secretary he'd ever had.

Miss Reedy's Summer Spectacular went off without a hitch. Jacinta and Sloane sang a fabulous duet and the concert was a fitting end to the year. With Caledonia Manor set to house the senior students in the new term, the last weeks of school were some of the happiest anyone could ever remember.

And as for the holidays, there was still some debate about what the girls would get up to. Aunty

Gee had mentioned that perhaps Alice-Miranda might like to spend some time with her at the palace. Sloane asked Alice-Miranda if she could take some friends along too. There's still a little time to decide.

Cast of characters

Winchesterfield-Downsfordvale Academy for Proper Young Ladies Staff

Miss Ophelia Grimm	Headmistress
Aldous Grump	Miss Grimm's husband
Mrs Louella Derby	Personal Secretary to the Headmistress
Miss Livinia Reedy	English teacher
Mr Josiah Plumpton	Science teacher
Howie (Mrs Howard)	Housemistress
Mr Cornelius Trout	Music teacher
Mrs Doreen Smith	Cook
Charlie Weatherly (Mr Charles)	Gardener
Elsa	Stablehand

Students

Alice-Miranda Highton-Smith-Kennington-Jones	
Millicent Jane McLoughlin-McTavish-McNoughton-McGill	Alice-Miranda's best friend and room mate
Jacinta Headlington-Bear	Friend

Sloane Sykes	Friend
Madeline Bloom, Ashima Divall, Ivory Hicks, Susannah Dare, Danika Rigby	Friends

Sainsbury Palace School Staff

Mrs Mildred Jelly	Headmistress
Professor Crookston	Science teacher

Others

Aunty Gee	Queen Georgiana
Constable Derby	Local policeman, married to Louella Derby
Myrtle Parker	Show Society President and village busybody
Reginald Parker	Husband of Myrtle
Hephzibah Fayle	Friend of Alice-Miranda's and owner of Caledonia Manor
Henrietta Sykes	Sister of Hephzibah and step-granny of Sloane Sykes
Ambrosia Headlington-Bear	Jacinta's mother
Silas Wiley	Mayor of Downsfordvale
Ursula	Silas's personal assistant
Stanley Frost	Owner of Wood End

There are more thrills ahead in
Alice Miranda's next adventure

Alice-Miranda in Japan